THE WATCHERS

Also by Helen Cresswell

Posy Bates, Again!
Meet Posy Bates
Time Out
Moondial
The Secret World of Polly Flint
Dear Shrink
The Piemakers
A Game of Catch
The Winter of the Birds
The Bongleweed
The Beachcombers
Up the Pier
The Night Watchmen

THE BAGTHORPE SAGA
Ordinary Jack
Absolute Zero
Bagthorpes Unlimited
Bagthorpes v. the World
Bagthorpes Abroad
Bagthorpes Haunted
Bagthorpes Liberated

THE WATCHERS
A MYSTERY AT ALTON TOWERS

HELEN CRESSWELL

Macmillan Publishing Company   New York

Maxwell Macmillan International
New York   Oxford   Singapore   Sydney

This story is a work of fiction and none of the
characters in it are based on real people.

First American Edition 1994

First published by Viking, London, England.
Printed in the United States of America
10   9   8   7   6   5   4   3   2   1
The text of this book is set in 12 point Bembo.

Library of Congress Cataloging-in-Publication Data:
Cresswell, Helen.
The watchers : a mystery at Alton Towers / by Helen Cresswell. — 1st ed.
p.   cm.
Summary: Two runaway children hide out in a theme park and become enmeshed
in an unearthly battle between the forces of good and evil.
ISBN-0-02-725371-6
[1. Runaways—Fiction. 2. Amusement parks—Fiction. 3. Friendship—Fiction.
4. Space and time—Fiction. 5. Magic—Fiction.] I. Title.
PZ7.C8645Wat 1994
[Fic]—dc20   93-41683

This story is for homeless children, everywhere

PROLOGUE

Here there are two worlds: the world of the day and the world of the night. So there are everywhere, you might say—the two worlds of dark and light. In the countryside the whole world is swallowed by the dark, except on moonlit nights when it is bathed in a cold, unearthly whiteness. In towns and cities and suburbs the sky and moon and stars disappear altogether, bleached out by the wide, unwinking glare of sodium lights.

Everywhere nights are empty. In the country nothing stirs but blown bough and bat's wing. You hear only the occasional bark of a fox, the owls hooting. Even in the city the people vanish as if in the twinkling of an eye. Here and there a cat streaks along the gutter. In shop doorways there are mutters and coughs and stirring from huddled shapes under boxes and rags. Night is the kingdom of the cat, but it belongs, too, to the homeless.

Here, at Alton Towers, there are those two worlds of day and night just as anywhere else, but—something more than that. By day, except in the winter months, it is the giant funfair of every child's dreams. The monorail shuttles back and forth, back and forth, bringing the visitors from their cars, which by midmorning are parked in shining acres. The whole wide valley is spinning. All day long the great, sighing swish of the Thunder Looper echoes through the valley. Perhaps there is bird song, but it is drowned by the screams as the Corkscrew hurtles, and the Alton Beast.

But at night . . . what happens then? Nothing, you might say, except that everything simply—stops. The families stream homeward, the last car leaves the now-deserted fields. Alton Towers is suddenly and enormously hushed, waiting for tomorrow and for the whole giddy cycle to begin again.

So you might think. But ask those who work here—because although Alton Towers might seem a place of magic, it works by nuts and bolts, and is staffed not by genies, but by flesh-and-blood people who clock on and off and have homes to go to at the end of the day. They will tell you stories, rumors. You will hear of the dolls in the museum that have been found in the morning, time and again, arranged on the floor in a perfect circle. (The museum has been locked all night. Dolls do not move of their own accord.) You will hear of a gray, cloaked figure gliding at twilight through Her Ladyship's Garden. Others will swear to having heard the legendary Talbot hound baying to the moon.

Speak to the security staff, the men who patrol that great wooded valley from dusk till dawn. These are men who do not jump at shadows. They will tell you of guard dogs stiffening, the fur of their backs standing on end at some unseen presence in the Towers or orangery. They will admit, too, that at night the place becomes strange, other, with the huge, brooding shapes of the silent rides, the intricate dark pathways of the garden. It is not the same place; it is a different place.

Come with me into the hushed valley on a still May night. We will tread softly, talk in whispers. The moon comes and goes and the lake yawns black and silver. What was that? A figure, long-legged on stilts of shadow, darts ahead and is gone. Above us the floodlit orangery seems to float in space. And listen—surely . . . surely not the faint music of a harp. And look—a strange, flickering white fire somewhere in the depths of the garden!

Dare we go further? If we step into that shadowy garden, we are surely going into a haunted place. Safer to turn back, back to the world of light and warmth and other human beings.

But if we go on, if we dare to take a risk, then perhaps we shall find a story. Let us go. . . .

ONE

"I'll run away, I will!"

"Where to?"

"Anywhere! I hate it here! I hate Gary and Steve and that smelly Rogers. An' I hate Mr. Foster and he needn't think I want his rotten sweets! There!"

A slick of colored shapes shot from his fist and scattered on the linoleum in a little rattling shower.

"He gave you them?" Katy was incredulous. She knew that Mr. Foster sometimes beat the boys—she had thought that was what was happening to Josh in there. He had only broken a window, and even that had been an accident, but boys had been beaten for less.

"I wish he was dead; I do!"

Josh's voice was muffled now. He was facedown on his bed—to hide the tears, Katy guessed. She stooped and started picking up the sweets. She opened the drawer of his locker and dropped them in.

"You needn't put 'em in there 'cause I shan't eat 'em!"

Katy sighed. The low sun streamed through the grimy window, making an unlikely halo of Josh's tufted hair. She hated the long evenings, supper over, nowhere to go, nothing to do. She could hear the rest of the boys, the ones who hadn't broken the window, still kicking and yelling in the yard below. The girls would be watching the television or huddled in some hideaway, smoking. There were hours to fill yet between now and bedtime. Time itself seemed a prison.

Josh shot up suddenly. "Let's run away!"

His face was grubby and smudged with tears, but so suddenly hopeful and alive that she was bound to smile.

"Wish we could."

"We can! Course we can! I done it before!"

He had, too. Katy knew that. He'd run away from the last home. His two younger brothers had been sent to a foster mother, leaving him there alone. Now here he was at Kirby House, and still alone.

"Got caught though, didn't you?" she said. "Caught and sent here."

He made a face. "Smelly hole!"

That, too, was true. Kirby House did smell. It was one of the first things Katy had noticed. It smelled of polished linoleum and disinfectant and boiled cabbage. It didn't exactly smell like a hospital, but almost. It certainly did not smell like home.

"Anyway, I shouldn't do it till after the weekend," she told him.

"Why not?"

"Alton Towers, silly!"

"Oh, *yeah*!" He had forgotten, really forgotten, even though he'd thought and dreamed of nothing else for weeks. "Hey, when you go into that Black Hole they take your photo! Terror!"

He went into an impression, arms stuck out rigid, eyes popping, and froze like that. Katy giggled.

"Hey—and you know something else? People *vanish* in there!"

"Dream on!"

"They do! They go in and never come out again—Rob told me. He *knows* someone who did! Tell you what—wish old Foster'd go in and vanish! Pff! Gone! Whizzing around in outer space!"

He jumped off the bed and did an impression of that, too, and Katy laughed, and that was the end of talk of running away—for the time being.

All the same she thought about it, that night in bed, waiting for sleep. Last week they had watched a video of *Oliver!* and she had thought then that Kirby House, if not exactly the workhouse, was not much better. And she herself, though not exactly an orphan, was one for the time being. Oliver had run away. He had been penniless. She had quite a lot of money—over twenty pounds—hidden in her duffle bag. Oliver had been alone. She would have Josh, who might be only nine, but had plenty of good ideas and certainly made her laugh.

Someone was crying, sobs muffled by bedclothes. Someone was usually crying at night. Sometimes it was Katy herself. No one took any notice. It was an unwritten rule. Everyone was entitled to cry in the dark and no questions asked. Even Oliver, she remembered, had cried sometimes.

Everyone at Kirby House went to Alton Towers. They went in a chartered bus belonging to the local charity—it was their annual treat. It was less than twenty miles and you could get there on an ordinary bus and be dropped off right outside. Some of the older kids were boasting how many times they'd been before.

On the way there Mrs. Rogers gave them the lecture they had already heard about twenty times. They were to go around in pairs; no one was to go on the lake without a grown-up. They were to make for a certain meeting point if they were in any trouble, and were all to meet at half past twelve for their packed lunch.

"You smaller ones, of course, won't be allowed on some of the rides without a grown-up. I shan't be going on them—I've no head for heights at all—but see Mr. Clarke or Mr. Foster. You'll all be given a map when we go in, so there's no need for anyone to get lost."

"Wish she would," Josh muttered.

Then they were there, and it was amazing—a whole new world in that wooded valley. From the monorail bringing them from the parking lot they could see it spread on all sides: the Haunted House, the Log Flume, the Big Top, and the Octopus. There were acres of space and green; places to get lost, escape.

Katy had not been altogether looking forward to the day ahead. She remembered a fairground ride she had once been forced to go on because her friends wanted to.

"Go on!" they had said. "Not chicken, are you?"

She had not wanted to be chicken but had soon found that she was. She could still remember the sheer terror of it, the speed and sickening lurches, the certainty that she would die.

"Let's you and me stick together," she had said to Josh, and was half ashamed of her motives. He was only nine and small for his age and a cast-iron excuse for going only on the tamer rides.

They were off the monorail and streaming toward the turnstiles, whooping and yelling.

"You two—you come along with me." It was Mrs. Rogers. She already had one of the smaller kids in tow. "Katy, did you hear me? Chips?"

"Chips" meant Josh—a lot of them called him that, and he hated it. He stopped and turned, and Katy held her breath. He couldn't throw one of his tantrums, not now, with the day hardly begun! He was scowling, all right, glaring at Ma Rogers with hot eyes. But none of the real danger signs were there—the thrust-out lower lip, the clenched fists.

"Come on—race you!" said Katy swiftly, and to her relief he nodded and ran.

Ma Rogers's voice came after them. "Now then, you two—wait! You hear me?"

At least they were not going around in a crowd, all twenty of them. Katy hated that. It marked them out. They might as well have CHILDREN'S HOME written on their T-shirts. No one could possibly take them for a family, or even a group of friends, all mixed ages, sizes, and colors as they were.

Now, just the three of them, with Ma Rogers trailing behind, they probably looked like any other family. They merged into the crowd.

"Though I hope no one thinks she's my mum!" Katy said to herself. And for a fleeting moment she thought of her own mother, a mother drowned in tears. She would have hated all this—the noise, the color, the screams and laughter. Toward the end she had stayed in bed all day, the curtains drawn.

"Come on!" Josh was tugging at her arm. "Look—animals!"

He'd never had a pet of his own—he couldn't, in the concrete apartment block he'd lived in. But he was always coaxing the Kirby cat, making it wriggle and pounce after things tied to a piece of string.

So they saw the animals. Then there were rides, and they all tried everything until they had worked their way around to the Towers itself.

"'S haunted!" said Josh. "Full of spooks!"

It seemed quite likely, even in the hot sun. Katy gazed up at the stone towers and turrets and mullioned windows that made it look part castle, part church.

"Wonder what it's like at night!"

"Full moon!"

"Bats . . ."

"Owls . . ."

They raced toward it.

"Wait! Katy! Chips!"

Mrs. Rogers wanted to look around the gift shop. "I've stood and stood while you went on rides till my legs ache. It's my day out as well, you know." She was in there for what seemed like hours.

"Why can't she go to the shops in Stoke?"

"Boring old bat!"

"Look—ice cream!"

They bought one each and stood licking. Then Mrs. Rogers came up behind them, and that was when the day went wrong.

"I never! And just before your lunch!" She took a swipe at Josh; he jumped back, and she got the ice cream instead. It went flying, and in the same moment Josh's face screwed up and his fists clenched and—

"*You!*" He kicked, hard, and got her full on the shin. "You! I hate you!"

He pelted off. Katy hesitated only for an instant and went after him. He ran straight ahead and followed the path into the gardens.

I'll never find him if he gets in there, she thought, and yelled, "Josh! Josh—wait!"

He didn't, but he did take a quick look over his shoulder before diving out of sight among the thick shrubbery. And as he did so, Katy saw something. It was the strangest thing. She saw a great black flapping shape like some enormous bird falling out of the sky. It came out of nowhere and flap-flapped in a wide, curving flight and dipped behind the trees and was gone.

"Landed!" Instead of fear she felt a sudden wild, unreasoning joy. The world had changed. She was on the edge of a mystery. "Josh!"

She saw him standing stock-still, staring at where that black shape had disappeared.

"You see that?" His face was still streaked with tears. (When he had a tantrum he cried at the same time, fury and misery mixed.)

"What was it?"

"Dunno. Dracula?"

She laughed and he looked at her, and for a moment she was afraid that she would have *her* shin kicked. But he grimaced, then set off again, kicking his feet and muttering. She followed.

"I suppose . . . we'd better go back."

"I ain't."

"She'll kill us!"

"Let her. What was it? Dirty great thing!"

"Not a bird."

"Giant bat!"

"That's about the nearest," Katy agreed. "Except you never get bats that big."

"Might, here," he said. "Give us a lick!"

She handed over her ice cream and he had more than a lick, and the pair of them wandered further into the gardens. There was hardly anyone about. Katy liked that. One of the worst things about Kirby House was the feeling of being hemmed in. From the minute she woke right through till bedtime, she was lucky to get even a few minutes alone to remind herself that she *was* herself. Sometimes she felt that she could hardly breathe, that even the air about her was invaded by other people.

"It's nice," she remarked.

"Look at that greenhouse—big as Buckingham Palace!"

"Conservatory," she said, consulting her map. "I call it orangery—sounds nicer."

"Yeah—makes you think of oranges."

They began to explore the gardens, which was not what they had come for at all. Yet it felt curiously right, and there was a kind of safeness and peacefulness that made it feel almost like home.

But children who visit Alton Towers do not usually spend much time in the gardens—not, at least, until late in the day when they have had their fill of rides and excitement. These two were the only ones there, and one person, at least, found that interesting. They were being watched—watched and followed.

"Look at this!"

"The Refuge," Katy read from her map. It was a small cave, a stone room. "Look—a proper little fireplace! You could live here!"

They followed a winding network of narrow paths. The watcher went after them, sliding from cover to cover, white-faced, yellow-haired, and long-legged as a crane.

Once, hearing familiar voices, they had to hide, crouching behind huge boulders. "Old Foster!" They watched him pass with his jerky stride, head slouched, hands in pockets. For once, invisible and unsuspected, it was as if *they* had the power. They beamed hate at his retreating back.

"Hey!" said Josh, tilting his head and gazing upward. "These stones—Stonehenge!"

Katy consulted her map.

"Yes! But not *really*—not here!"

She too tilted back her head, and the stones filled the sky, and for an instant she was dizzy and seemed to feel the earth tilt under her feet. And in that instant she thought she heard children's voices, very faint and far-away, singing.

"Ugh!" She shivered and shut her eyes for a moment as if to break a kind of spell.

"What's up?"

"Nothing."

"Lunch," said Josh. "I'm ravenous!"

In the end they decided they would give the picnic a miss. If they went back now, they would probably be told they didn't deserve any lunch, and almost certainly be sent back to the bus for the rest of the day. It would be perfectly possible to go through the afternoon without running into anyone from Kirby.

"Get a beating anyhow," said Josh gloomily. "Might as well make it worth it."

They carried on up through the gardens, then came down in the Skyride. At the bottom there were warm smells of food.

"I've got enough to buy something," Katy said. "Oh, Josh!"

He had darted off and retrieved a paper dish just dropped into a bin. The next minute he was wolfing its contents. He was not called Chips for nothing.

"That's disgusting!"

"'S not! Nothing the matter with 'em!"

Suddenly daring, she snatched a chip herself. He was right. It was still warm, even.

"Disgusting!" she said again. "Come on—let's buy some!"

And so they did, and wandered back through the

gardens, eating them. The watcher had kept track of them and was still there, keeping his distance, keeping out of view.

"Better than a moldy packed lunch!"

"*And* we haven't got to look at Foster's ugly mug!"

"And listen—we can go back and have some more rides!"

The others would be safely out of the way for at least an hour now. The pair went on one ride after another, and finished off by going back up on the Skyride. From their bird's-eye view they scanned for any sign of the others.

"Can't see them."

"Vanished in the Black Hole!"

For the rest of the afternoon they ducked and dived, seeing familiar figures from a distance, never close enough to be spotted themselves. The game added an extra excitement to the day. And all the time, without their knowing it, another game of hide-and-seek was being played. The watcher was tireless, he stalked them patiently, hour after hour.

As six o'clock drew near they grew quieter. That was the time they were due to meet at the monorail to go back to the bus.

"Let's stay here!" Josh said. "Hide! They'd never find us!"

"Course they would. They would in the end."

"I s'pose so."

"They can't kill us."

"They can nearly."

They were in the gardens again, among the friendly,

sheltering green—a green that concealed themselves and gave cover, too, to that secret watcher.

"Have to go back," Katy said. "No point in making things worse."

They went in silence, dreading what lay ahead. On a seat among the rocks they passed an old lady, dressed all in dusty black, at her feet a couple of bulging bags. She watched them, eyes intent and dark. Katy had a curious, fleeting impression that she was there waiting for them, expecting them.

"See that?" hissed Josh. "Bag lady! What's she doing here?"

"Sh! She'll hear you!"

"See *her* on the Thunder Looper!"

"Must be someone's grandma." Though Katy did not really believe that. Nobody's grandma looked quite like that.

Then they were out of the gardens. The lake lay shining ahead, and beyond that, the monorail station. The moment of reckoning had come.

TWO

It was even worse than they had feared. And it went on longer. It was not like an ordinary row that flares and then is over and done with, forgotten. It was as if they lived under a brooding, poisonous cloud.

"They hate us," Josh said. "And I hate them."

Even the other kids cold-shouldered them. The staff had been badly rattled during the hours Katy and Josh had been missing. They took it out on everyone, as if to say, "Don't *you* go getting any ideas. In the end you'll be caught. And we run this show."

So when Josh, after a few miserable days, said again, "Let's run away!" this time Katy agreed. She had thought of it before he had, and had even worked out where to go. It was beautifully, blindingly simple. The idea flowered fully grown in her head from the seed sown, without her even knowing it, that day at Alton.

They would catch an ordinary bus to Alton Towers. They would pay to go in, like everyone else, and then they would disappear. They would not vanish into thin air, of course, in the Black Hole. They would simply

23

become invisible. Alton Towers was swarming with children, thousands upon thousands of them.

"And we could go on rides, all day every day!"

"And they'd never find us!"

Not on this occasion. If they had tried to disappear last Saturday, they would have been found before nightfall. Everyone knew they were in there, somewhere. Now Alton Towers was perhaps the last place on earth anyone would think of looking.

"There's bags to eat—and I've got some money!"

"So've I," she told him. "Over twenty pounds."

Josh counted his—eleven pounds, twenty-three pence.

"But most of it will go on getting in," she warned.

Josh was used to scavenging; he'd done it most of his life. He remembered the warm chips from the bin. It seemed to him that at Alton Towers food grew on trees.

"What'll we do at night?"

Katy had thought of that. "Remember the gardens? That little cave—the Refuge?"

"And that great greenhouse!"

"Orangery."

"Slept in a bandstand last time I run off. There's one of them as well!"

They laid their plans. They would do it the next day.

"Put warm things in your bag," Katy told Josh, already being mother. "And any eats."

She knew that Josh hoarded food like a squirrel. He did it out of long habit. He nicked it from the table, the pantry—even, she suspected, from shops. He nicked and hoarded anything that was going—except chips. These he scoffed as if he could never get enough of them. There were chips galore at Alton Towers.

The pair stuffed their bags ready for their long camping. Neither of them thought of how long that might be. They were escaping from misery into a glorious, fun-filled freedom that seemed to stretch ahead forever. They fairly fizzed with excitement. Katy felt so electric that she thought she might even be giving off sparks.

"Better look miserable at supper," she warned. "They might guess."

Josh pulled his face into a fiendish scowl, and Katy laughed.

"You'll be told to wipe that look off your face!"

He was, too.

That night Katy lay awake for a long time. Where shall I be this time tomorrow . . . ?

It was beyond her imagining. She and Josh were running into a strange new world, a world for which no one had ever prepared them. They would be explorers. The biggest adventure ever!

Just before she drifted into sleep she remembered fleetingly the black, flapping shape that had dropped from the sky into the gardens that day. But in the dreams that followed she was not pursued by giant bats or a leering Dracula. She was somehow held and sheltered under a warm cloak, safe.

They had already worked out their plan. It was easy. Before breakfast, when the coast was clear, they darted out and hid their bulging bags behind the laurels by the gate.

"If they see us go out with 'em they'll smell a rat," said Josh, already wise in the ways of escape.

They had breakfast. Josh wolfed his down and Katy saw him deftly nick the usual toast. She herself could hardly eat and had to force herself to swallow. Not that anyone would have noticed. On the whole no one noticed her much at Kirby House. She tried not to look at Ma Rogers or any of the others in case they read her secret.

She was scared. She admitted it, but it did not occur to her to change her mind. She was venturing into an unknown world, but not from a snug, familiar nest. Kirby House was as foreign and unsafe as anywhere she might be going.

After breakfast they picked up their packed lunches from the table at the end of the dining room. They were only minutes away from freedom now. All they had to do was to keep acting normally. They often walked together to school.

"Hang around!" Katy heard Josh mutter from the corner of his mouth. There were seven others who went to the same school. No one must see them standing there.

She went back up for the last time to her room. Three of the beds were made neatly enough, but Debbie Farmer's, as usual, was a mess. Automatically she went over and straightened it, then stood uncertainly. She was used to filling time, trying to make it pass.

Now this five minutes seemed an eternity. She sat on her bed. For the last time! she told herself, and was glad of it.

She sat, just sat, without even looking about her. She did not want to remember that room.

"Here, what's this?" It was Mrs. Rogers peering in to check the beds. "Not skipping school—don't you think it, miss!"

"No—oh, no! I just—I'm just going!"

She fled. Josh was ahead of her, himself evidently having been flushed out of hiding. Down they went, through the empty hall and out into the fresh air, away from the dreary smell of polish, the smell of misery itself. Then they retrieved their bags and were on the road.

"All gone now, I think," Josh said, meaning the other kids from Kirby.

Their relief did not last long.

"Watch it—the Kirby kids!"

"Mums don't want 'em!"

"Shove 'em in Kirby and slam the lid!"

"Kirby crawlers—creepy crawlies!"

Raucous laughter. Swipes from satchels and bags. They were used to it. Mostly Josh retaliated, to their delight. Not today. He trudged doggedly on, though Katy saw the telltale signs, the clenched fists.

When they had gone, she said, "We hadn't thought. *No one* must see us at the bus stop—not just the kids from the house."

"Have to hide somewhere till they've all gone!"

Josh ducked down a narrow alley and Katy followed till there was a sharp elbow bend and they were out of sight of the main road.

"Wait here, I s'pose!" Josh kicked his sneakers against the wall as he would have against his tormentors' shins if they were there.

They waited twenty minutes, just to make sure. Punctuality was strict at their school, but there was sometimes the odd straggler. The bus stop was only two minutes away, but they had no idea how long they would have to wait.

"Thank goodness there's no one else waiting!" Katy meant no grown-up, who might wonder what two children were doing out of school—might even watch them, and notice where they got off. She had a sudden inspiration. "Look, you run down to the next stop!"

He stared.

"So's no one sees us together! When they do start looking, they'll be looking for two of us."

"What if the bus comes before I get there?"

"Get on the next one. I'll wait at the other end. Got your money?"

He nodded and tore off.

"And don't sit next to me when you get on!" she called after him, though she was not certain that he heard. Surely, anyway, he would have the sense not to. That was the whole point of it.

She watched him go around the corner and out of sight. She turned back and saw, to her horror, a bus approaching. It was the one! It drew up, and she climbed on. She thought, He's going to miss it; he's going to miss it!

She paid her fare, deliberately fumbling, playing for time. It was no use. They passed Josh, still running, a good hundred yards short of the next stop. He looked desperately over his shoulder, and for a fraction of a second their eyes met.

"I'll wait for you!" she mouthed, but could hardly hope the message was received. But it's better, she told herself. If we're not even on the same bus, it's better.

She wished now that she had run on and let Josh catch the bus. After all, she was older. He, on the other hand, was tougher; she knew that. He was streetwise, used to fending for himself.

The dirty town gave way to green. Town child as she was, that in itself marked a change, the beginning of something.

> How many miles to Babylon?
> Three-score miles and ten.
> Will I get there by candlelight?
> Yes, and back again.

She had not the least idea in the world why that old rhyme came into her head. She seemed to hear it, her own younger voice chiming with that of her mother as they pored together over the old book. She could even see the picture, all blue and white and gold, full of stars. The green through the glass went into a blur as silly tears rose to her eyes. Mum was all right once. And she will be again.

In the meantime, Alton Towers was just a place to go to, like Babylon. Though we shan't be back by candle-light.

Nor would she and Josh be safe in a nursery-rhyme world between the covers of a book. The real world was a cold and drafty place.

When the bus drew up at Alton Towers, she was the only one to get off. The driver hardly seemed to glance at her. All the same, instead of going straight in through the wide gateway, she started to walk toward the village. In case he sees me in his mirror, she thought, and was pleased with her cunning.

As soon as the bus had disappeared she turned back. Cars were turning into the drive, one after the other. If she just stood there, by the time the next bus came hundreds of people might have noticed her—thousands, even. Not that I'm particularly noticeable.

She was glad that she did not have bright red hair, or a long yellow perm like Debbie Farmer's—something that people might remember. Mousy is safe.

All the same, it would be better if she could get rid of the bulging bag. She walked through the gateway and saw that nearby there was shrubbery with dense, shining leaves. I'll wait till there are no cars coming, then dive in there!

Her chance came almost at once. She ran and plunged into the rhododendrons, their rubbery foliage brushing her hands and face. Then she was in a safe hidey-hole. She could smell the leaves and the soil and was suddenly back in her old garden, years ago, playing hide-and-seek. For hours she would crouch, or so it seemed, waiting almost with terror to be discovered.

This was real hide-and-seek.

And it could be a whole hour before the next bus. More, even.

She pushed her way through to a small clearing, dumped her bag down, and sat on it. She could hear the *whoosh, whoosh* of cars turning off the road. When a bus drew up she would be able to hear it, the steady throbbing of the engine behind the wall.

She sat and waited, and slowly, slowly the world shrank to a dim cocoon. All the time she could hear the regular sighing breath of the Thunder Looper. It was hard even to imagine the brightness and color out there. The longer she sat, the less she felt like ever venturing out again. It reminded her of those days when you would wake and then pull the blankets high over your head, unwilling to face the day. There had been a lot of those lately.

Glad I didn't come on my own. If she had, perhaps she would have ended by going back on the next bus.

She kept looking at her watch, though somehow that kind of time did not seem to apply there among the rhododendrons. They had their own clocks of night and day, spring and summer—a long slow march of time with nothing to do, nowhere to go, just being. She actually shut her eyes and tried to feel what it must be like to be a plant, or tree. She turned her toes into roots and put out her arms for branches. There was a rustle close by and she blinked her eyes open. It was a bird. She watched it dart and peck, dart and peck, and was glad of its company, and pleased that it did not seem to mind her. She held her breath and stayed motionless, still being a tree.

Fooled it proper! It'll build its nest in me next!

Then she spoiled it all by snorting at the thought, and the bird flew off. In the same moment she heard a bus.

Quick!

She left her bag and pushed her way out and was just in time to see the bus pull away. There he stood, a small familiar figure, looking uncertainly about him.

"Josh!"

He turned, and his face lit up.

"In here—quick!"

She dived back into the shrubbery. The next minute he was there with her, so close that she could smell the potato chips on his breath.

"Anyone see you?"

"Nah! Easy!"

"We're here! We've done it; we've done it!"

They clutched each other and did a jig of unholy joy, there among the springing leaves. A shower of birds flew out.

"Look, we've got to plan it."

"Go in one at a time."

She nodded. "And get rid of these." She meant the bags, suspiciously bulging, as if they held packed lunches for five thousand. In any case, they were too heavy to lug around all day.

"Where?"

"In the gardens. Heaps of places we can hide them there."

"What if someone finds 'em and pinches 'em?"

"They won't. They haven't come here just to crawl about in the bushes!"

He grinned. "We have!"

"Got your money to get in?"

He rattled his pocket. "Me first, this time."

"I'll stay here five minutes, then follow. Meet you in the gardens."

"By that big greenhouse."

"Orangery."

He was gone then. The leaves closed behind him.

She decided to watch her second hand all the way around the dial, five times. She had never done that before, and it was as good a way as any to pass the time. It was curious. The first minute went quickly, but the second slower. The third went more slowly still, and by the time the needle hand was making its fourth circle, it was as if time itself were coming to a stop.

Like watched kettles never boiling, I s'pose.

One day, she promised herself, she'd try to do it for a whole hour—half one, anyway—and see if time actually *did* stand still. There seemed no reason why not.

It was strange to be climbing aboard the monorail on her own, so soon after that first trip only a few days earlier. It was crowded, but no one took the least notice of her. All the same, her heart thudded as she alighted and made her way to the ticket kiosks.

What if it's children only accompanied by an adult! The thought had only just struck her. She could hang around, she supposed, till she saw a family, and ask if she could go in with them. She'd done that often enough at the cinema. But then they might remember. *My picture could be on TV, and they'd see it and tell the police!*

She hung back, watching. There was no sign of Josh. *He* must've got in.

There was no rule about grown-ups. She could tell that by the jostling lines of kids at the kiosks. What were they doing off school? Were they on school outings, or special birthday treats? It didn't matter. The point was that they were buying tickets, then rushing off and through the turnstiles. She joined one of the lines, willing herself to look extra mousy.

Then she had a ticket in her hand, and was through the turnstiles and into the park. She was even clutching another map of Alton, though she had saved hers from Saturday and brought it with her. *Find my way twice as well now!*

She did not need the map to find the gardens. She went through the paved courtyard with its blaring band and turned left. On one side was the broad shine of the lake with its fake swans, on the other the Log Flume and paths leading to the Haunted House. Ahead she could see the sun striking fire from the glass of the orangery. Josh would already be there, waiting— munching his way through his provisions, as like as not.

She turned into the gardens and already felt that she was home. It was a great green maze where they could go their own secret ways. Blackbirds flew low across her path. A faint haze hung over the valley, a heat haze.

In the distance a cuckoo called, and she thought she heard running water.

She was passing great, rearing stones, fixed and ancient, old as time. She had a swift memory of that other day when she had stared up at them and become dizzy. And heard children—singing—could've sworn I did!

Suddenly she wanted to run and press her cheek against that cold and powerful stone and tell it of her coming. It would be a kind of sign. These were the kings of the valley, and she and Josh intruders. They were not ordinary, careless visitors who came and went, glancing and laughing. They had come in deadly earnest, to be accepted into that kingdom and learn its laws.

And so she ran toward the towering stones and dropped her bag and clasped one, and was instantly glad. It was the strangest thing, to hug stone. She shut her eyes and felt her cheek go cold, and slowly became aware of the true, deep stoneness. She felt it coming powerfully through her outstreched arms, her head, her whole body. It was harder than anything she had ever known, and cold beyond all coldness. And beyond the coldness were the children's voices, not singing, but laughing, shouting. Yet they were so faint and far-away, were so curiously echoing, that even now she wondered if she was really hearing them, or whether they rang inside her own head.

It might have been moments she stayed like that, or whole minutes. She moved only when she knew that she had properly met the stone, had it in her bones.

She did not know that she was being watched.

At last she opened her eyes and stepped back, and in that instant another figure slid swiftly out of sight. Dizzy, cheek numb, she turned to where she had dropped her bag, then made for the orangery.

She stepped inside, and the air was suddenly different and warmer. She found Josh right at the far end, sitting on the ground, legs outstretched.

"Thought you were never coming!"

"Sorry." She said nothing about the stones.

He scrambled to his feet. "Let's get going! Ditch these!"

They went out and found a secret place, deep in foliage.

"And our jackets," Katy said. "Leave them as well. We'll be boiled. I'm going to keep my money in my pocket."

"Why? 'S all right here."

"Have you got yours?"

"Only a couple of quid left."

"Well, take it."

"Already have."

Back on the path they turned and inspected the shrubbery. There was not so much a glimpse of the hidden bags.

"Whoopee! We did it!"

Again they performed a little dance of joy, drunk with their own success.

The watcher, in his own hiding place, saw and smiled.

Out of the gardens they were just like any other day-trippers with the freedom of the park. No need now to separate, not be spotted as a pair. They slipped invisibly among the hordes of other children tumbling and running in hundreds, thousands. Here they went on one ride, there another. There was no hurry. They had all the time in the world.

"Wonder what that lot are doing now?"

They were on the miniature railway. Katy knew what he meant and looked at her watch. "Had break!"

"Singing in the hall with old Nowchil!" Mrs. Beardsley, the music teacher, began everything she said with "Now, children . . ."

It was hard to imagine her, miles away, strumming away as the lunch ladies clattered behind the hatches and everyone deliberately sang wrong notes. They should be there, but they were here. Would they have been missed yet . . . ?

They were among strangers, and that made them anonymous. There was not a single person to see them, greet them, and later remember them.

Except once. They were by the Undertakers and making for the Black Hole. Josh, thwarted because he was too young to enter it himself, had announced his intention of checking his theory.

"Kids *do* go missing in there," he insisted. "Told you—Rob knows someone who did. That's the whole point of black holes."

He intended to watch that line. He would count them all in and count them all out.

Katy tugged at his sleeve. "Look!"

It was the dusty old woman, the bag lady of their

first visit. She was coming toward them, and now that she was upright they saw that she was bundled up not in a coat, but in a long, flowing cloak. So unlikely a figure was she among that multicolored throng that she could only be dressed up as part of the Alton scene—escaped from the Haunted House, perhaps. Why, then, did she fix the pair with her fierce, bright eyes; why did they feel that it was they she had come to find?

Both, without saying a word to each other, held their breaths as they passed. Josh took a backward look over his shoulder.

"Here again!"

"What's she *doing* here?" It was unimaginable.

"Dressed up?" Josh suggested. "No one goes around looking like that."

"Bag ladies do. I've seen them in town."

"So where'd she get the money to get in?"

Katy did not know.

"And what's she come for? *She* ain't going on the Beast or the Corkscrew. Give her a heart attack!"

It was true.

"Out of the Haunted House, I bet, and going for her lunch. Tell you what—I'll do the Black Hole later. Let's go and get our sandwiches."

"No." Katy had thought about this.

"'S nearly time."

"We'll need them tonight."

He stared. "Packed lunches at night?"

"What else would we eat? Everywhere'll be shut, remember."

Josh, she realized, had not thought of this—she

doubted whether he had thought of anything, such as small details like where they would even get a drink once the park had closed, let alone where they would sleep. Josh was used to surviving from minute to minute. The future hardly existed for him.

"Right then—let's buy something."

"The money won't last long," she warned.

"Go around the bins then!"

Katy grimaced. She had thought about that, too. Her mother was not particularly fussy about germs, but some people were. On the other hand, she did not see how germs could get into chips or pizzas just by their being dropped into a bin. One minute people were eating them, the next they were in the bin. It was as simple as that.

"Or nick something!"

Now she was shocked. Lots of the kids did, she knew. Most shops around had notices about only two children at a time being allowed in. Other bigger ones had notices: THIEVES WILL BE PROSECUTED.

"The bins," she said.

It was not so easy as they had thought. The picture of bins full of still-warm chips and pizzas soon faded. On Saturday they had evidently struck lucky. For one thing, the bins were still almost empty.

"Expect they're leaving their lunches till late. Case they throw it all up again."

Josh craned and peered into a bin. "Not much in there."

"Looking for something, sonny?" It was a man, one of the attendants in Alton Towers red.

Katy walked on, trying to look casual and nothing at all to do with it.

"Dropped an apple in by mistake," Josh said.

"I should leave it. Wouldn't fancy it even if I fished it out—not when it's been in that lot."

The man walked on. After that they were more watchful. They darted here and there among the kiosks, watching people buy food, trailing them, willing them to leave some and toss it in a bin. All the while delicious smells of chicken, chips, and doughnuts wafted past.

"I'm ravenous! Come on, let's just buy some chips."

"No," said Katy firmly. "We've got to save the money for emergencies."

"This *is* an emergency." He clutched his stomach and groaned. He really did eat vast quantities of food for one so small.

"*Real* emergencies. We'll go and get our lunches."

The bags were still there in the hiding place.

"I'm only eating half mine," said Katy, watching Josh gobble his. "There's tonight, remember."

But tonight seemed a long way off there under the hot sun, and he munched steadily on as if there were no tomorrow, let alone tonight.

THREE

The park began to empty, slowly at first, then as six o'clock approached, fast. They were in the Towers, exploring the vast rooms with their high ceilings and stone windows.

"'S for giants! Giants must've lived here."

"Could we sleep in here . . . ?" Katy was dubious.

"Haunted, I bet. Full of spooks."

It seemed likely.

"There's the orangery and a bandstand and—hey, that little cave place."

The Refuge.

"More fun out there, anyhow. Proper camping."

"Look, they're all going home." She was looking out over the lake. From all sides people came streaming, making for the monorail. Their shouts and laughter drifted up. They were tired and happy after their long day, and now they were heading for home. She and Josh were already home.

"Better get back to the gardens," she said, "or it'll look funny, us going there when all the rides have shut. It's nearly seven."

And so they went back to the gardens, by now almost entirely in shadow. Above them the Skyride was still running, from sunshine above to shade below. Shading her eyes and looking up, Katy remembered that black shape flap-flapping down out of the sky. It had not seemed frightening at the time—merely strange. But at night . . . ? She pushed the thought away.

By now the shrubbery where their jackets and bags were hidden was as familiar as a cupboard under the stairs. They could use it every day now, Katy thought. If the bags had not been spotted today, they wouldn't be tomorrow, or the day after, or the day after that. She pushed that thought away, too. Was it really possible that they could live here, day after day, for weeks, months even? And then what?

They ate the remains of their sandwiches and Josh fished out a packet of potato chips for each.

"I'm thirsty."

"Same here."

They looked at each other.

"Should've thought of it earlier, and bought something," Katy admitted.

"Did you know you die of thirst before you starve?"

"What d'you mean?"

"It's true. You can last *ages* without food—weeks. Think of all them hunger strikes. But you got to have water."

She blinked at him, ever so slightly scared. Was it true? And how long before you began to die of thirst?

"Always go down to the lake, I s'pose. Ugh!"

"Or drink the dew from the leaves."

"There isn't any dew, idiot."

"Will be, in the morning."

"I'm thirsty *now*!" He jumped up. "Must be a tap somewhere!"

"Oh, yes, in someone's kitchen!"

"In the gardens. Always is, in parks. Water the flowers."

His past experience as a runaway was coming in useful now. Not that his powers of survival had ever been so severely tested before. He had always been in town, where there were corner shops open till late, garages, and outbuildings you could nip into.

"I'm going to find one!"

"Careful!"

"Why?"

"It's past seven. If anyone sees us now, we're done for!"

The pair stared at each other. This was the real moment when they began to be on the run. For the first time they had a whiff of danger.

"They'll have missed us—"

"Reported us to the police—"

"Our pictures could be on TV—"

This was all true, but there in the fast-cooling valley, that other world of Kirby House and stale smells seemed unreal, even impossible. Could it all still be going on—the ball being aimlessly kicked in the yard, the curtains drawn against the low sun streaming in on the television?

Then they noticed the silence. The rides had stopped, the daylong hum of machinery, the mingled screams and laughter. It was eerie. They had lived all their lives in towns and never known such silence. There was only the echoing evening whistle of birds. They heard the hollow call of the cuckoo somewhere out of sight on the wooded slopes.

"Ain't it quiet!" Josh whispered, and suddenly shivered as if someone had walked over his grave.

"Look out!"

A red-coated figure was weaving through the garden below. As they watched, it stopped, then scanned about as if searching.

"Looking—for us!"

"Can't be! How can he?"

It was a relief when the figure carried on walking and went out of sight.

"The sheriff of Nottingham!" said Josh.

"What?"

"Pity we're not wearing Lincoln green. Spot us a mile off in these."

"We're not exactly Robin Hood," Katy pointed out. "We're not robbing the rich to feed the poor. We *are* the poor."

"Living in the greenwood, though. Pity there's not a hollow oak. Look, let's find that tap!"

Katy was rummaging in her bag. She found what she was looking for, a navy sweater, and pulled it over her head. "Camouflage," she said.

"Lincoln green!" Josh in turn delved in his own bag. It crackled as he did so. Stuffed with potato chips, she guessed. No wonder he was thirsty. He found a black sweatshirt, then pulled out his tongue and panted like a dog. "Water! Water!"

They found a tap, sure enough, in the orangery, and noisily slurped water from their cupped hands.

"Buy drinks tomorrow and keep the cups," Katy spluttered.

"Or bottles."

"We can wash here, as well."

"*Wash?*" He blew out a shower of spray.

"Course. We'll get filthy."

"Who cares!"

"You will, when you start to stink! Not to mention people noticing. Didn't you bring any soap?"

"Course not!" He was contemptuous.

"Well, I did. And a washcloth and toothbrush." She wished now she had checked the contents of his bag.

"I reckon we could sleep in here."

"Mmm. Not exactly cozy. All those windows!"

"What d'you expect? Curtains?"

She had to laugh, picturing long falls of velvet. "All right, we'll try it."

She was now aware of a more pressing problem. "I want to go!"

"Go, then. Plenty of bushes."

And so she did, leaving a patch of gently steaming earth. "But what about when we *really* want to go?"

"Do it doggy. I did." He was showing off. He was a world-class runaway.

"It'll only be at night, anyway. Plenty of proper toilets."

At half past nine they took their bags up to the

orangery. It was not yet dark, but they wanted to be properly settled before it was.

"Got a flashlight," Katy said, "but better save it for emergencies."

"Emergencies!" he scoffed. "Like what?"

She did not know.

The dim air of the orangery was still distinctly warmer than that outside.

"Better wear our jackets, though," Katy said.

"Using mine as a pillow."

Either that, or rest his head on a crackling bagful of potato chips, she thought. A folded sweater served as her pillow. They stretched out and lay there, gazing up at the glass roof. It was infinitely strange. The ground was hard, and there was a cold, metallic, geranium smell. Katy could not pretend to herself that she was in just another room, another bed.

"Shall we actually be able to sleep?" she wondered.

"Don't half feel funny," Josh said after a while. "Never slept in an orangery before."

"Well, shut your eyes and try."

She closed her own. She pictured her mother's face, as she always did before falling asleep. She saw it not as it had been in the last year, but as it had been in the days when she had still been smiling. It was a kind of magic, a way of changing things.

"Good job Micky and Kev ain't here!" said Josh. He was evidently doing the same, conjuring up his absent family. "Never get them sleeping here, no fear!"

His little brothers were by now no doubt safely

tucked up and dreaming. Micky, the youngest, was only three.

"Oh! What—"

"Flaming Norah!"

They shot up, dazzled and blinking. The orangery was flooded with white light; the glass was blazing.

"Run for it!"

They scooped up their things and bolted, heads ducked, though it was pointless even to try to hide in that searching light. They fled into the gardens and the welcome dark.

"Nearly shot me out of my skin!"

They gazed back at the floodlit orangery, seeming to float now above the twilit gardens.

"That's that, then."

"Sh!"

They listened. Someone else was in the garden. They heard voices, then footsteps. Breath held, they crouched among the bushes.

"There!" Josh breathed, and pointed. Below were the shadowy figures of two men, one with a leashed dog.

"Patrol!"

They waited until the men disappeared before they dared move or speak.

"Dog!" said Josh hoarsely. "Blooming great Alsatian!"

The gardens at night were more dangerous than they had guessed.

"Now what?"

"Dunno."

"We can't stay here. Not all night."

"I know! The bandstand!"

They could still make out its shape in the near darkness.

"It'll do. Slept in one before."

The bandstand was less of a goldfish bowl than the orangery, but colder. The smell here was fusty, mingled with the strong night odors of earth and green. Again they arranged their makeshift pillows and settled.

"You asleep?" came Josh's whisper, after a time.

"Yes—are you?"

They both giggled.

"Yeah—fast on and snoring!"

There was a long silence. There were only the faint sounds of night—rustles, the far-off hooting of an owl.

"My mum ain't suitable. Not a fit person."

The words came bleakly out of the darkness. Katy did not know what to say.

"I bet she is, really," she urged.

"That's what they said when we went in care. 'Not a fit person.' What's it mean?"

"Don't know."

"That why you were sent to Kirby?"

"My mum gets depression. She gets it really bad."

"What's that?"

"You know—really sad. All the time. Crying, and that. Not getting out of bed."

"Who got you your dinner then?"

"Me, silly. Got hers, as well. Not that she ate it. I did everything, really."

"What? What sorts of things? Go on, tell us!"

"You know. Washing clothes and that. Cleaning—"

"Won't have to do that here!"

"No. Hey, that's the best thing about here—no cleaning. Scrub the grass, dust the trees. . . ."

"Where's she now, then? Your mum?"

"Hospital. She'll get better. Where's yours?"

"Dunno. But I expect she'll come for me."

"Course she will."

"I get this amazing dream—had it lots of times. An' she comes and fetches me—right out of Kirby! And we go to this house—dead posh it is, with a garden, and there's the other two, and there's this slide, and they're bashing up an' down it, and then they see me, see, and—"

"What?"

"Nothing. That's it."

She waited, but he meant to keep the ending of his dream to himself.

"Sweet dreams!"

Again she closed her eyes. Almost at once she thought she heard music and wondered whether she was already asleep and dreaming.

"Hear that?"

She sat up then. It *was* music, falling in ripples over the dark wooded valley.

"What is it?"

"Sounds . . ." She was trying to place it—not a violin, not a flute— "Sounds like a harp!"

"Harp? Angels play harps!"

So they did. The notes were so round, so gold and perfect, that they might be dropping straight out of heaven.

"Oh—and look!"

She caught his sleeve and pointed, and there, on the other side of the valley, were sparks of light flying.

"Fireworks!"

"No—look, it keeps coming and coming!"

It was an endless cascade of cold white stars dancing to the time of the music.

"What *is* it?"

They gazed up wide-eyed, enchanted and terrified. It was a wonder.

All day long the near impossible happens at Alton Towers. You can dare a haunted house, go around the world in eighty days—vanish into a black hole, even. But this was impossible beyond all that. It was as if they had reached the rim of the world and tumbled off.

They clung to one another, dizzy, and as they gazed, their eyes grew heavy. They were being charmed to sleep. Wordlessly they groped for their makeshift beds and lay down. Their lids drooped; the music chained them. They were asleep.

They were sleeping soundly in the shadowy bandstand in those vast gardens while the world went on. Behind drawn curtains in a million homes the television beamed out pictures of two children, a boy aged nine and a girl of eleven. There was a shot of Kirby House, an interview with Mrs. Rogers.

The children, she said, were, so far as she knew, perfectly happy. No, she could not think of a single reason why they should run away. Yes, the boy had done so before, but that was because he had just been separated from his brothers and was upset. He had got over that now. She thought that they would probably be back by morning.

No one mentioned a trip to Alton Towers, a dropped ice cream, a kick on the shins, and the punishment that followed. And so, as Katy had guessed, the last place on earth that anyone dreamed of looking was Alton Towers.

FOUR

Josh awoke first. The smells of dew on fern and earth were so strong that it was as if his nose had woken him. Then he remembered. He sat bolt upright and shivered. Katy lay nearby, curled like a cat and breathing softly.

"Katy!" he whispered. She did not stir. He scrambled to his feet and went out of the bandstand and into the morning.

"Brr!" He shivered again. The light was flat and gray. Dawn, he supposed. What time was that? He did not know. Someone at Kirby House had pinched his watch. But it don't matter!

What did matter was that he was hungry. He fished a handful of crackers from his bag and noticed that his supplies were getting low. Better get stocked up! He did not know exactly how. There was certainly nothing here in the gardens, except worms for early birds. He set off for the kiosks and the bins.

Something fast and silver streaked across his path. A squirrel! He tracked it with his eyes. The leaves rustled and shook, charting its progress. Ain't it *fast*! It was the first squirrel he had ever seen. It might as well have been a kangaroo, or a leopard, in its strangeness.

He decided then and there that he would tame it, have it as the pet he'd always longed for. It would run to him and sit on his shoulder—he could almost feel the soft brush on his neck. There was another rustle, closer. He turned to see another squirrel scampering under the bushes. It stopped and swiveled its head, and for an instant its bright black eyes met his own.

"Hey, come on, come on!" he coaxed softly. "Don't be scared!"

The squirrel posed, tilting its head.

"'S only me!" But he could not resist taking a step forward, and the squirrel bolted. It was gone in a flash.

He carried on, disappointed, but curiously honored to find that he had now shared a home with these wild silver things. They would get used to him in the end, he thought, take him for granted as one of the family.

He reached the wide path he had to cross and paused, looking right, left, and right again. Just like crossing the road!

Here, if anywhere, was where he might be spotted. To his right was the Towers itself, now thinly washed with early sun. As he glanced he saw, or thought he saw, a face at one of the upper windows. Then it was gone, as if someone had stepped swiftly back out of sight.

He ran, ducking into the bushes ahead.

I only *thought* I saw someone! Can't've, he decided.

He emerged from the bushes into the area by the Dome. There were the kiosks, blind and shuttered: the

American Doughnut, Specialty Fries, and Fish and Chip Pullman. He sniffed hopefully, but the only smells were those of the morning itself, cold and fresh. Darting forward, he peered into the nearest bin. Empty!

He guessed that the others would be, too, but he checked all the same. He went around the back of one of the kiosks. And so he came upon his third squirrel, and this time it did not run; it did not even see him. It was sitting, cool as a cucumber, nibbling at a doughnut held between its paws.

He stood, hardly daring to breathe, and watched. He did not know which enchanted him most—that he should have found food, or that he should have found a squirrel eating it. He stood for what seemed ages, watching that solitary breakfast. And when the squirrel did go, it was not because of any move made by him. It simply dropped the doughnut, twitched its nose, and vanished.

Josh stared at the half-eaten doughnut. Hungry as he was, he drew the line at eating a squirrel's leftovers. But where's it from?

Where there was one doughnut, there might be more. A large plastic sack stood by the back door of the kiosk. There was a tear in it, and through that tear he could see . . .

Doughnuts!

It was unbelievable. A sackful of them! He snatched one and started to cram it into his mouth. He had not realized he was so hungry. He ate another, then another. Then he stuffed one into each pocket, and, carrying

54

as many more as he could hold, dived back into the bushes.

When Katy awoke she could not, for those first moments, think where she was. She was aware of cold; of fresh, stinging smells; of bird song right by her ear, it seemed. She sat up and looked over to where Josh had been and saw that he had gone.

"Josh!"

Her stomach curled sickeningly. This was an adventure she would never have dared alone. She scrambled to her feet and stood combing the valley for a glimpse of him.

"Josh!" she called, but her voice came out as a croak. She dared not call louder. There had been men in the gardens last night, with a dog, and—

That music! She remembered that the darkness had been filled with those eerie notes, and how white sparks had swarmed like bees. That it had been a kind of magic, she could not doubt. Had the valley filled with unseen presences as they slept; could Josh have been spirited away, as changelings were in the stories? Her head felt fogged and slow.

He'll have gone off somewhere, she told herself, looking for food.

Even this was risky, dangerous. What if he had gone looking for pickings, and been spotted and caught? She looked at her watch. Six o'clock. The entire valley was silent, deserted. It was almost impossible to imagine that within only a few hours it would be thronged and noisy, a day like yesterday and all the other yesterdays.

There was not a sign of a single other human being.

Katy shivered. She looked back at the bandstand, littered with their things, then out again at the still gardens. Suddenly making up her mind, she swiftly put her own things together and concealed them in the bushes. She did the same with Josh's and then, drawing a deep breath, began to march toward the place where she guessed he would be.

As she went she thought how strange, how foreign, the world seemed. She was in an early morning such as she had never known before, had never even guessed at. All her other awakenings had been in curtained rooms, little stuffy worlds of their own. She tried to imagine her bedroom at home, with its clown mobile and poster-covered walls. It seemed a million miles away and impossible.

Then she saw the bag lady. She stopped dead, staring.

The old woman sat on a bench as if she had sat there all night gathering dew. She sat so motionless that she might have been a tree or a stone. It would have been no surprise to see the silvery tracks of snails on her rusty skirts.

For an instant Katy was tempted to turn and run. That bag lady had been stalking them. She had singled them out.

Then the old woman turned her head and was looking straight into Katy's eyes. It was too late now to run. She was held by that hard gaze, locked.

"G-g-good morning!"

There was no reply. Instead, the bag lady shook her head, slowly, as if in warning. She shook and shook it, on and on.

"What—what d'you mean?"

Katy was mystified, alarmed. If only the old woman would utter a word, just a single word, she would shrink to human size, become manageable.

"I don't understand!"

Not a word. Not a sign that she had even spoken. Just the slow shaking of that grizzled head under its drooping hat.

Katy could bear it no longer. She dropped her eyes, broke the spell. Then she ran, ran until she was out of breath and as far as she could get from that inexplicable meeting.

By now she was almost at the edge of the gardens. It was somewhere around here that the music had come from, and the lights.

Even now, in broad daylight, she shivered at the memory. She shivered, too, at the thought of that old woman mysteriously coming and going across their path. Surely she could not have sat all night on that seat? Surely she could not live here?

Cautiously she crossed the wide path by the Towers, where Josh had gone before her, and all at once she saw him ahead, coming toward her.

"Josh!" she screamed, and ran to meet him. "Where've you been? Oh, I was—"

"Sh! Keep your voice down, will you? Quick—back in the gardens!"

They crossed the path again together, in full view of the Towers. They did not know that they were being watched.

"Here—have one!" He thrust out his hands, brimming with doughnuts. "Better hot of course, but . . . I've had three!"

She took one, but did not eat it.

"Listen, there's bags of 'em, and you'll never believe—"

"The bag lady!" She could not wait to hear his news before telling her own.

"The what—oh!"

"She's there again! In the garden!"

Josh was only momentarily taken aback. He had not seen that fierce gaze, that slowly shaking head. "So what?"

"But why? *Why*?"

"See you?"

"Of course she did! She—she knew I was coming; I swear she did! And—and—" She faltered, knowing how impossible it was to convey the menace of that meeting. "She was . . . sort of warning me!"

"What about?" Josh spoke thickly, into his fourth doughnut.

Already they were being followed. A long-legged figure stalked them, jumping from bush to bush.

"How do I know? Oh—you aren't *listening*!"

"I am, then!"

"Wait!" She clutched his arm. "She was just around that corner."

She tiptoed forward, and Josh followed. She peered past a branch and saw the seat—empty.

"Gone!"

She did not know whether she was glad or sorry.

"There you are, then! Listen, you'll never guess . . ." And he told her how the squirrel had led him to the hoard of doughnuts.

"Just sat there having its breakfast!"

They had reached the bandstand, and stopped dead. There sat the bag lady, watching them.

"'S her! She knows!"

This time the bag lady did not shake her head. She pointed—straight at them, or at something immediately behind them. Katy half turned—too late. The stalking figure stepped swiftly out of sight.

Now the bag lady's eyes were fixed on Josh's hands, and the doughnuts.

"She's hungry!" Katy whispered. "Give her one!"

"They're all we've got," he whispered back. "Might have to last us all day."

Katy realized that she was still holding her own. She stepped forward.

"Here," she said awkwardly. "Have this!"

It seemed a very long time before an old, veined hand stretched out to meet her own. It took the doughnut and withdrew under the dusty cloak. There was no thank you, but there was a strange softening of that wrinkled face, those dark eyes.

"Do you—do you live here?" asked Katy, emboldened.

There was no reply.

"In that little refuge place—that where you live?" Josh asked.

"We've come to live," Katy told her. "You won't tell, will you?"

There seemed little likelihood of this. The old woman remained stubbornly dumb. She seemed to hear, but either could not or would not speak. Some-one else heard, and remained silent.

"We'll be going, then." They had no reason to go, and nowhere to go, but Katy knew that the bag lady would stay put. The bags were hidden nearby. They must go away, then come back later when it was safe.

"See you!" said Josh encouragingly.

"Oh—I've thought of something!" Katy turned back so swiftly that she almost—almost—caught sight of that other watching, listening figure. "Last night—did you hear that music?"

"See those lights? Dead weird it was!"

But now she was not even looking at them, let alone listening. The bag lady seemed to have an invisible cir-cle around her, a circle into which no one could step. It was the silence that made it.

Josh shrugged. "Come on. Rude thing!"

"Sh!"

They trudged on toward the bandstand, and behind them sprang that other figure, white-faced and yellow-haired and long-legged as a crane.

Katy found herself unreasonably glad to have met the old woman again and given her the doughnut.

"Listen," she said, "she might be an old woman like the one in fairy tales."

"What one?"

"You know—the old crone. And she's begging for a crust and the young man gives it to her, even though it's all he's got in the world."

"Well, that doughnut ain't all we've got in the world; there's a sackful up there—a sackful! What young man, anyway?"

"You know—the prince, or the youngest brother, or the woodcutter's son. And then she turns out to be a fairy in disguise and gives him his heart's desire!"

"*I* don't know any stories like that. Anyhow, *not* a story, this ain't. And I think she's dead rude, the way she never answers. If we did that, we'd get whacked."

Katy said no more, partly because she did not know how to put into words what she felt. It was more than simply being glad that she had given her doughnut to the bag lady. It was to do with hidden meanings, mysteries.

"What day is it?"

"Wednesday."

"Sure?"

"Course."

"Tell you what," Josh said, "we'll have to make a calendar."

"A what?"

"You know—so's we don't lose track of time. It's what prisoners do—hostages—they make notches in their cells. They do it for years!"

They had reached the orangery, and he eyed it speculatively.

"You're not to carve on that!"

"Okay. Someone might see it, anyhow. A tree . . ." He looked about for a suitably calendar-looking tree. "No—I know! On them stones—Stonehenge!"

"No!" She was shocked at the sacrilege. She had felt the cold power of those stones run into her bones. "Look—that tree there!"

"Oh—right!" He took out his knife and carved a *W* on the ribby bark. "That's for today. Then—just a notch, see—no need to do a *TH*. Now all we've got to do is make a notch every day. Simple."

He ate another doughnut in celebration. Then his eyes suddenly widened. "Our things!" he choked. "In the bandstand! What if she's took them!"

"I hid them, silly," Katy told him. "We'll take them back to where we hid them yesterday. Safe as houses there. But we can't get them till she's gone."

And so they killed a little time, then made their way back to the bandstand. They went warily as they drew nearer. They were stalking the bag lady, and at the same time they themselves were being stalked by that other person, white-faced, yellow-haired, and long-legged as a crane.

FIVE

"I'm beginning to feel like a doughnut," Josh said. "I'll end up with a hole in my middle."

They had moved their bags from near the bandstand, back to the original hiding place.

"Your teeth'll all drop out. Specially if you haven't brought your toothbrush."

"I reckon there could be bags of different food all over the place. Tell you what—let's see if there's any spuds."

"Go now, you mean?"

"Course. While there's no one about."

It seemed a good idea. Katy herself felt that she could not face a daylong diet of cold doughnuts.

They went to the orangery to drink from the tap, then crossed the garden again toward the Towers.

"Listen!" said Josh suddenly.

"Cars!"

"But they ain't allowed in!"

They ran to where the gardens bordered the lakeside path, and peering out saw that vans and trucks were everywhere, crisscrossing the network of roads.

"What're they doing here?"

"Dunno. But we'll have to keep to the gardens."

"We can still get to the potato place—only got one road to cross."

But when they reached the area by the Dome, the trucks were there before them. They crouched in the bushes, watching.

"Collecting the rubbish!" Josh whispered. "Look—there go the doughnuts!"

The torn sack was heaved out and tossed with a pile of others.

"Bang go our spuds!"

They retreated through the shrubbery.

"At least we'll know tomorrow," Josh said.

"The early bird catches the worm."

"And the early squirrel catches the doughnut!"

They were back in the gardens.

"Where was that music coming from last night?" Katy said.

"And those lights. Didn't dream 'em, did we?"

"You know we didn't."

"Any case, don't suppose you can have two people dreaming the same thing."

"Twins might, I s'pose. If it happens again tonight, we'll notice where it's coming from."

"Go and look, you mean—track it down!"

Katy said nothing. She was not sure that she would have the nerve.

Automatically they had made their way back to where their things were hidden—or where they thought they were hidden.

They were still there, but so was something else. Tucked into the strap of Josh's rucksack was a large, torn piece of paper. They both saw it at once. On it were printed just two words: WATCH IT.

The shock was enormous, stunning. Someone knew they were there, was watching them. Their secret place was not secret.

"I—I don't believe it!" said Josh at last.

"Oh, Josh—I'm scared!"

"Who *is* it?"

"It couldn't—not—not the bag lady!"

They stared at each other, hardly believing what had happened.

"She was at the bandstand!"

"But why? Why should she?"

They did not know.

"But she wasn't there when we got back."

"Could she have been hiding? Saw us move 'em?"

Katy shook her head. "I don't think it was her." She did not know why she thought this. It was simply that she could not imagine the old woman hiding in the bushes, peering, watching. She never made any attempt to hide—rather the opposite. She seemed almost deliberately to put herself in their path.

"Now what?" said Josh bleakly.

"We'll have to find a new hiding place. Think—whoever it was could've *pinched* them!"

Those bags contained all they had.

"How"—Katy lowered her voice—"how do we know we're not being watched *now* . . . ?"

"Could be anywhere, whoever it is," Josh admitted.

The gardens, which had seemed so sheltering and safe, had at a stroke become a dangerous jungle, a place where hidden eyes were watching their every move.

"Just have to keep our eyes peeled," he said. "I know. We'll run, really fast, then whiz around and look!"

If they were being pursued, they would then at least see their pursuer. Katy's heart hammered. She was not certain that she wanted to see whoever had scrawled that brief warning.

"Come on—let's do it!" Josh picked up his own bag, and Katy followed suit. "We'll make for that Chinese thing by the Skyrail. Run—run fast as you can, and when we're out of breath we'll stop and whiz around. I'll give the signal!"

Katy already felt that her legs would hardly stand, let alone run. She nodded dumbly.

"Right—now!"

He was out and running, and Katy followed. Along the narrow, winding paths they tore, and they ran faster, certainly, than the bag lady ever could. But they ran not knowing who was at their heels—if anyone at all. They ran propelled by terror until their lungs were bursting and Josh gasped, "Now!" and they stopped and swung around in a single movement.

The path behind them lay deserted. No one was following.

"Quick!" Josh ducked into the bushes, and Katy followed. They stood there, brushed by leaves and twigs, and gasping for breath.

"No one . . . saw us!"

"Stop . . . here a bit!"

They pushed their way further into the greenery and found a wide space where they could drop their bags and sit.

"So from now on, we'll leave our things here," Josh said.

"And every time we come here, use a different path."

"And keep checking behind us."

They had only really been playing at hide-and-seek till now. Now it was in deadly earnest.

"I don't think we should sleep in the bandstand again," Katy said. "Anyone could see us. Even those guards with the dogs."

"We could make a sort of den, in among some bushes."

"Get some cardboard boxes—"

"And newspapers!"

"Ugh—and then get all soggy when it rains!"

"Did you bring your umbrella?"

They stuffed their hands in their mouths and rocked with mirth.

"Here," Josh said. "We could sleep here!"

They were surrounded by dense bushes, and looking up saw that they were roofed high up by an overhanging tree. It was a safe green den, secret.

"Good as anywhere!"

And so it was decided. During the day, in between having rides and scavenging for food, they would also look for newspapers and keep their eyes open for any large boxes.

"I bet there's loads behind those shops and food stands!"

"Then fetch 'em tonight, when no one's about!"

"We'll come out at night like foxes!"

"And badgers!"

"I'm Mr. Fox!"

"And I'm Mrs. Badger!"

When they finally emerged from their hideaway, it was with extra caution. They peered out from behind the springing leaves and checked that the path was clear in both directions. It was here in the gardens that they were at their most visible. Once in the park proper, among the hordes of other children, they became invisible, perfectly camouflaged.

Now the rides had started, the daylong hum and whir, threaded with screams and laughter. All morning the pair went from ride to ride, sometimes singly, sometimes together. Toward lunchtime they had a stroke of luck in the form of a complete hamburger, still hot, not even touched.

"Little monkey!" A woman slapped a small girl. "If you felt sick, why didn't you say so? Wasting my money! Come on!" She went off eating her own food, and the child went after her, leaving the hamburger on the seat.

Josh was there in a flash. He tore it in half and handed part to Katy. "Bingo!" he spluttered through a mouthful.

"You ever nicked stuff?" he asked when he had finished.

Katy shook her head.

"What—not even from old Carter's?"

Old Carter kept the newsstand by the school.

"'S easy! Specially here. Aren't even keeping a lookout like old Carter."

"I don't think I'd be any good at it."

He eyed her thoughtfully. "I'll do it."

"Oh, ought you?"

"Told you. Easy."

"I've got enough to buy a bottle of drink—we need the bottle, remember."

"Nah. No point paying. I'll get it. You go . . . I dunno . . . to the Log Flume, and I'll meet you there. Got to keep moving."

He sped away. Katy watched him go, then went and bought a bottle of orange soda. She was wandering toward the Log Flume when she saw the bag lady.

Again! It was unnerving, uncanny.

The old woman was not even looking at her, and yet Katy knew, quite certainly, that it was for herself she was waiting. Coming toward them was a young man wearing Alton red.

"Excuse me . . . ?"

He stopped.

"I wondered . . . that old woman . . ." She pointed. "Is she out of the Haunted House?"

"What old woman's that, love?"

"There, on the seat."

He glanced over. "You putting me on?"

"No—honestly. I just wanted to know."

"Sitting there, you say?"

"Yes. Is she dressed up?"

"Dressed up? Not dressed at all, if you ask me. See-through. Invisible. Nice try, kid!"

69

He went off, hands in pockets, whistling. Katy stared after him, mystified. What did he mean, *see-through, invisible?* He surely could not have meant that he saw no one. She looked over again to where the old woman sat, solid and breathing and plainly there—properly there.

"It's a mystery," she said out loud. Then, to the bag lady, boldly, "Look, are you following us?"

No reply.

"It wasn't you that left that note, was it?"

No reply.

"Because if it was, it was a rotten trick! We're not bothering you, so don't you bother us!"

She ran then. She did not stop till she reached the Log Flume, and only then did she look back. The seat was empty.

Gone! Almost at once she wished she had not spoken those words, wished she could take them back. She thought again of the old crones in the fairy tales, and shivered in the hot sun. Glad I gave her that doughnut, though!

She sat and waited for Josh. He came carrying a plastic bag. In it he had bread, bottles of drink, cheese, tomatoes.

"Easy! You just nip around the backs to the kitchens!"

"But what if you get caught?"

He shrugged. "Run for it. 'S only bits and bobs—they'll never miss it."

"It's stealing, though."

"Look, it ain't a crime to steal when you're starving.

That squirrel with the doughnut—that wasn't stealing. That's what we're like now—squirrels."

Katy supposed he was right. "Mr. Fox."

"And Mrs. Badger."

"Listen, I've got something to tell you."

"What?"

"The bag lady . . ."

"Seen her again?"

"Yes, but . . . that's not all. I think—oh, you'll never believe it—I think she's invisible!"

He boggled, mouth crammed.

"I asked this man—I was trying to find out if she's out of the Haunted House—and . . . I don't think he could see her!"

"Dream on! Did he *say* he couldn't?"

"No, not exactly, but—"

"Course he could. You gone potty or what?"

She had not supposed that Josh would believe her.

"Let's go and take the rest of this stuff to the den. I can empty it out and keep the bag in my pocket, case I need it."

"And make sure no one's been there."

"Come on—we'll go different ways. See you there!"

He was off. Katy followed more slowly. The nearer she came to their hideaway, the more her steps dragged. What if someone *did* already know it? What if there was another scrawled message? Worse still, what if their things had gone . . . ?

In their office two security officers were watching the news. "Concern is growing for the two children who disappeared yesterday from the Kirby House Children's Home. Interviews with other children from the home have revealed that there had been an incident, last week, on an outing to Alton Towers—"

"Hear that?"

"—for which they were being punished. . . ."

"Poor little devils!"

"How do kids end *up* in places like that?"

". . . hospital, receiving treatment for depression. The mother of Joshua Grey has not yet been traced. Police are appealing to her to come forward."

"There you are! Don't even know her own kid's missing. I ask you!"

SIX

It was twilight, and Josh was growing restive.

"I'm going down there."

"We don't *need* any more food."

"I saw all these big boxes."

"We'll be all right as we are."

"*You* ever tried sleeping on soil? Any case, I *fancy* sleeping in a cardboard box. Be proper homeless, then."

"But if they're big enough to sleep in, you *can't* fetch them here—someone's bound to see."

Katy did not want him to go. She did not want to be left alone in the darkening valley.

"'S nearly dark. I'll be in the bushes most of the way. Mr. Fox goes hunting! I'm off!"

He pushed his way out of the shrubbery, and the walls of their den closed behind him.

He went swiftly through the cooling gardens, now and then checking over his shoulder. He was making for the Towers, its battlements and turrets visible against the streaked sky.

Once out of the gardens, he ran from one sheltering

tree or building to another. The spaces in-between were dangerous.

Every now and then, foxlike, he stopped and listened. Here and there he could make out the vast, dark hulks of the rides, like some strange, prehistoric beasts. They were eerily silent, yet intent, as if in waiting.

The boxes were still there, where he had seen them earlier, stacked behind the gift shop. He pulled at one. It was heavier than he had thought. Gently, very gently, he eased it down. As he did so, his foot struck an empty bottle, and it clattered over the stone. He held his breath.

A long-legged figure stepped swiftly out of the shadows, and Josh was grabbed from behind. A hand went over his mouth.

"Gotcher!"

Josh fought furiously, legs kicking, but his captor laughed softly, gripping him firmly with one arm, the other hand still clamped over his mouth. His assailant was not only pinning him, but dragging him away from the buildings and into the shrubbery.

"Might as well—leave—off! I've—got yer!"

With a sudden movement he released him and spun him around, one hand still tightly gripping his wrist. Josh opened his mouth.

"You yell, and they'll have us both!"

In the dim light Josh could make out a thin, pale face and long yellow hair. He closed his mouth, stopped struggling.

"That's better. Now—what's your game?"

"G-game?"

"You and that other kid. We've got tabs on you, don't you worry!"

"Who . . . are you?"

The youth grinned. "No harm you knowing. Ollie. Just call me Ollie."

"I mean . . . what're you doing here?"

"Same as you, I reckon."

"What—living here? Sleeping rough?"

"That's about it. But we're good at it, see. Been doing it months—years."

"What—*here*?"

"I'm asking the questions," Ollie told him. "What're you two doing here?"

Josh said nothing.

"Run off from home, have you?"

"Sort of. Children's home."

"Ah. Police after you, are they?"

"I—I dunno. Must be, I s'pose."

"Oh, yes. Minors, run off—they'll be after you, all right. Headlines on television, I shouldn't wonder."

"They'll never think of looking here!"

Ollie grinned. "Nice one, kid. But they are—looking. Now, me and my friend, they ain't looking for us."

"W-why aren't they?"

"Not minors. Old enough to go missing and not a question asked. Oh, no. Be murdered tomorrow and chucked in the sea, and there's no one'd come looking for me and my . . . friend."

"Where *is* your friend?"

"Ah, that'd be telling. We'll come to him later. He'll be wanting to see you."

"Look, can I go now?" said Josh. "We ain't doing any harm. Plenty of room for all of us."

"Oh, yes," agreed Ollie softly. "Plenty of room. And all of us safe as houses, as long as none of us gets seen. So you will be careful, won't you?"

"Course! We *are* careful."

"*I* knew you were there," said Ollie. "And so did—my friend." He gave Josh's arm a sudden wrench. "So—watch it!"

Katy, waiting in the den, was thinking that running away was not as simple as she had supposed. The actual running had been easy enough. It was all the other details that she had not foreseen. Things like getting food and water, finding places to sleep.

The position she was in now she certainly could not have imagined. Here she sat in a hidey-hole walled and roofed with branches. That was all right. She felt safe in there, certain of her own invisibility, like a mole in a hole or a fox in its den.

On the other hand—and this was the big thing—moles and foxes had things to *do*—or so she supposed they had.

> The fox went out on a chilly night.
> He prayed to the moon to give him light,
> For he'd many miles to go that night
> Before he reached the town-o.

That was what foxes would be doing, at this very minute—they would be off hunting, running fast as arrows, following their noses. Moles, of course, were meant to be blind, so how they spent their spare time was more of a mystery. She knew hardly anything about badgers, but she liked the look of them, and doubted if they were ever bored.

Or birds, she thought. Flying around all day whistling and making nests. Or squirrels.

She, on the other hand, was bored. This was the last thing on earth she had thought anyone could be on a runaway to Alton Towers. Already she and Josh had spent what seemed like hours and hours just sitting and waiting. But at least they had had each other to talk to. Now she was alone.

"If I *was* Mrs. Badger—what'd I be doing?" she asked herself out loud.

Shan't start talking to myself, she thought. First sign of madness.

She wished she had thought of bringing a book, though she doubted whether using her flashlight to read it by would count as an emergency. You could not actually die of boredom, even if it sometimes felt that way. If it had not been for that horrible scrawled note that morning, she might perhaps have plucked up courage to venture out and wander alone in the deserted gardens. But there could be eyes out there, watching. She idly picked a twig from an overhanging shrub.

What shall I ask . . . ? I know. Will Josh get caught?

She plucked the leaves off the twig one by one, as if it were a daisy. Caught. Not. Caught. Not. *Caught!*

She dropped the twig. Stupid thing! Only a game, anyhow!

But she was unsettled by the twig's prophecy; she

wished she had never asked it. She peered at her watch and could just make out its face in the gloom. She remembered how she had actually watched the minutes pass yesterday—was it only yesterday?—when she was crouched among the bushes, waiting. She remembered how simply watching it had seemed to make time pass more and more slowly.

She decided to try the experiment again. And this time I won't say I'm going to watch five minutes, or ten—I'll just keep on and on watching, and see what happens.

She did not really believe that time would actually stand still, that there was an edge of riskiness about the plan. But there was a curious unreality about her being there at all in that place. Here she was alone and away from all the everyday things that anchored her in time and space. There was just herself, the darkness—and time.

She began the watching. The tiny second hand moved steadily around the dial. It seemed almost like company, as the only other moving thing about her. By the time it had completed its first circle it was a friend, and she quite forgot her reason for watching it, and simply . . . watched. It went slowly and inexorably, making the pattern of time. Time was a circle . . . around . . . around. . . . Her head felt curiously light, and as if it, too, were spinning.

So far away did she seem that she was not surprised when she heard the music. It came tumbling and clear as a peal of bells. It seemed to beckon her.

She got to her feet and pushed her way through the

leaves. Forgotten now was the fear of watchful eyes. She stood uncertainly on the path and saw the lights, the endless dance of white blobs. They and the music were inextricably linked.

Katy began to walk toward their source, her eyes fixed and blind like those of a sleepwalker. And as she went, the nature of the light changed, expanded. Still white, it yawned and flared, yawned and flared like sheet lightning. She had to reach it, was drawn by that and the curling fall of the music.

Without knowing how, she had reached the stones, those same cold stones she had met only yesterday— was it yesterday? Now they were strangely lit against the dark sky.

She stopped then, and the scene before her was impossible and yet perfectly natural—expected, even. There, in that flaring light, sat an old man playing a harp. His hair and beard were white as wool. His hands ran over the strings and plucked out notes and light together, as if the sparks were music made visible. He did not raise his eyes or turn his head, yet Katy felt that he sensed her presence.

The music and the lights kept coming as if bubbling up from a bottomless well, as if they would never stop till the world's end.

Katy stepped forward. She stepped within the ring of stones, and the world changed in the twinkling of an eye. The night had gone; it was broad day. She was acutely aware of color: green grass, white daisies, yellow sun. The music rippled into silence. The man raised his head.

For an instant Katy's eyes met his; then she turned and fled. She fled from sunlight into the dark again, a silent dark now, the real dark of the deserted gardens.

Katy had forgotten the fear of watching eyes. That had been swallowed by the terror of miracle. She was running not from a human pursuer but from the impossible. She ran and ran and then, without warning, there was sudden light again. She screamed.

She was right by the orangery, floodlit and blazing, and silhouetted against it she saw Josh—and someone else.

She screamed again. She stood perfectly still and screamed. Then she was being dragged roughly forward, and heard Josh's voice.

"'S all right! 'S all *right*!"

There was another, unknown voice. "Shut *up*, will you!"

She shut her eyes. The unseen hands loosed their hold, and she sank to the ground. She opened her eyes and was half blinded. They were inside the floodlit orangery with its dry-geranium smell and glittering glass.

"What—what . . . ?"

Josh was crouched beside her, and opposite, almost level with her own, a wax-white face with holes for eyes.

"Just keep your voices down, will you!"

Katy stared at him, unable to guess who he was, what was happening.

"It's Ollie," Josh said. "He lives here as well."

"But—the light! They'll see us!"

"Not they," said Ollie. "Think a place is safe, if it's lit. Never look here in a thousand years. Slept here dozens of times."

"Your friend," said Josh. "Where's he sleep?"

"Ah," said Ollie. "That'd be telling. Give you a clue, though. He's the King."

"The . . . King?"

"And he's got some little jobs for you to do. Nothing much—a bit here, a bit there."

"I don't like you," Katy said. "Just leave us alone."

"*That's* not very nice," said Ollie. "Not very nice at all. Any case, you don't *have* to like me."

"Well, *I'm* not doing any jobs," she said.

"Oh, I think you will," he told her. "You're on the King's patch, see. Got to pay him rent."

"*He* doesn't own Alton Towers, whoever he is!"

"Oh, yes. King of the castle. Finders keepers. *We* were here first."

"We'd better, Katy," said Josh anxiously.

"Oh, yes, you'd better," Ollie agreed. "All it needs is a little note left somewhere. . . ."

"That note! You!"

He smiled. "A little note . . . something like . . . 'The two runaway kids are in here. Get the dogs out.' "

They stared at him in the searing light.

"Yeah . . . something like that. . . ."

SEVEN

They had spent their first night in the den among the bushes. Now, even that was not safe. Ollie knew of it. He had followed them there in the darkness, and repeated his orders. They were to fetch food, first thing, enough for himself and his friend—the King.

"We've got to, Katy," Josh urged.

"I hate him!"

"Look—I'll go and get the stuff. Then all you've got to do is come with me to take it to them."

"King!"

"But they're on our side."

"And you don't even want to *believe* what happened to me!"

"I do! But that doesn't matter. It's not—it's not *real*!"

"You're beginning to get on my nerves," she told him.

He grinned. "That's what my mum used to say! You sound just like my mum!"

"Well, I'm not. And if you hadn't gone down there last night—"

"They *knew* we were here! Look, I'm going to get some stuff—you can like it or lump it!" He jumped to his feet. "Mrs. Badger—too right! Badger, badger, badger!" Then he was gone, being Mr. Fox again.

He had snatched up his plastic bag and pushed his way out through the damp walls of their den. Through the dawn hush he went, eyes watchful, darting from cover to cover. The squirrels went slippery and silver ahead of him. He wondered again where they went in the daytime. Alton Towers, it seemed, was thronged with presences that came and went, with secret lives.

There were rich pickings today. He collected not only doughnuts, but pizzas, potatoes in their skins, bread. He crammed his bag because he was not collecting for two, but four.

On his return journey he went warily, jumpy in the knowledge that somewhere he would be waylaid.

"I'll be there, don't you worry," Ollie had said.

All the same it was a shock when that figure stepped out, on stilts of shadow in the early sun.

"Ah!" Ollie eyed the bulging bag. "Where's she?"

"Back in the den."

"Fetch her. You're going to see the King."

"Couldn't just I go? She—"

"Fetch her."

"I—I'll try."

"Give us that bag first. Meet me by the stones."

"But—but some of it's ours!" Too late—the bag had gone.

"And remember—all it needs is a little note. . . ."

Katy was incredulous when Josh told her.

"Where? The *stones*?"

"Come on—quick!"

"But that was where—"

Impossible to explain the power of the thing she had seen last night. Impossible to describe the terror of stepping out of darkness through some invisible circle and into broad day.

"That was last night! Come *on*!"

She hesitated. Part of her was filled with a deep, superstitious dread. The other part wanted, actually wanted to revisit the scene. Now, at dawn, would there still be echoes, glimpses, reverberations . . . ?

"Oh, all *right*!"

They set off.

"And don't go being rude to him again!"

"Shall if I like!" she told him.

Ollie stepped into their path as they reached the stones. Long and pale as he was, he seemed to have a gift for invisibility, for sliding in and out of view.

"Here we are, then," he said. "The King's waiting."

"If you think—" began Katy, but Josh gave her a dig and frowned warningly.

They followed Ollie. Katy went warily. A sudden thought made her catch her breath. The King! Could it be that snow-haired man who sat in a storm of light? Was she now to meet him face to face?

In among the rearing stones Ollie stopped. "Here we are, then," he said again. He raised his voice. "Here, chief!"

They waited. A figure stepped from behind a stone. Josh and Katy stared.

It was a youth hardly older than Ollie. His hair— half black, half yellow—rose like a stiff cock's comb—a crown. He had rings in his ears, his nose. His eyes were small and screwed against the sun. He stood, arms folded, surveying them.

"These are the kids," Ollie said. Then, "Tell him your names."

"Josh."

"Katy." Then, boldly, "What's yours?"

The youth smiled thinly. "No need to know my name. I'm King, see."

They were mesmerized by his presence, by his extraordinary appearance.

"Run off . . . from a home . . ." He said the words consideringly, as if their fate depended on them. "Could be handy. . . ."

"Course it is, chief," said Ollie eagerly. "You saw all that stuff! We can get hold of anything now."

"Er—could we have some back, please?" said Josh. "That was our food as well."

"Oh, plenty more where that came from."

"But the trucks'll be coming soon, to collect!"

"Chuck 'em a pizza, Ollie," ordered the King.

He rummaged in the bag and did so. Josh caught his, but Katy's dropped.

"I'm not eating *that!*" she said.

"Oh, hoity-toity!" said the King. Then, with menace, "Pick it up."

She looked at him, at the pinched face with its hard eyes under that towering crest.

"Pick—it—up!"

She stooped and did so.

"Now—eat it!"

She looked imploringly at Josh, but he averted his

eyes. She took a tiny bite from the crust, forcing herself to swallow it.

"That's better. Needs training, Ollie."

"Yes, chief."

"Show 'em the note!"

Ollie dug in his pocket and produced a folded square of paper.

"What does it say, Ollie?"

He read out, "The two kids run off from the home are here. They sleep in the gardens and the dogs will find them easy. Signed, a well-wisher."

There was a small silence.

"The pigs are after you," said the King.

"Too right they are!" chimed in Ollie.

"And if they catch you . . . then what?"

They stared at him. They did not know, had not dared think.

"Sent back there," said the King. "Or somewhere worse."

"I know, see," said Ollie. "I've been in homes, and—"

"Shut—up!"

"Sorry! Sorry, chief!"

"Your mouth's too big."

"Sorry."

"Say it!"

"My—my mouth's too big."

The King smiled. He looked again at Katy and Josh, from head to foot. "I'll leave 'em to you, Ollie," he said. "You know where to find me."

Then he had gone.

Ollie carefully folded the paper again and put it in his pocket, all the while watching their faces.

"Now," he said, "what about money . . . ?"

"Trust you to put all your money in the same place," said Katy bitterly.

"It was you that said it! You said not to leave it with all the other stuff."

"Well, I've still got ten pounds."

"He made us turn our pockets out!"

"I put it somewhere safe."

"Where? Up your knickers?"

"Never you mind."

She had folded the note tightly and pushed it between stones in the Refuge. She did not know why. She had always enjoyed hiding things, having secret places.

"You know who he's like, don't you?"

"Who?"

"The King. He's like Fagin. In *Oliver Twist*."

"And I'm the Artful Dodger!"

"Thought you were supposed to be Mr. Fox. We could always run away."

"We already have, stupid!"

"Go to that place for lost kids, and tell them who we are."

He stared. "You're joking!"

"It wasn't you that had to eat that horrible pizza!"

"I'll pinch you another—honest! I'll get anything you want."

"Not pinch—steal. 'S all very well for you—you don't *mind* stealing things."

"Go on—call me a thief!" His eyes were hot and bright, his fists curling. "Go on, then! Go on—see if I care!"

The danger signs were all there. She said nothing.

"Oh . . . I'm off to get some grub. You starve to death if you like!"

And he had gone. They had been sitting in the bandstand, sharing a bag of well-crushed potato chips. Now the rides had started; she could hear the hum, the steady swish of the Thunder Looper. Josh, she guessed, would work off his feelings by going on one after the other, yelling and shouting till he felt better.

Josh had not forgotten his ambition to tame a squirrel. He had already bought a packet of peanuts as a lure. He himself preferred salted, but was dubious about this, and so had bought the plain. It was no use taking anything from the sacks by the kiosks. The squirrels could help themselves to that—and that in itself was amazing. He watched all the wildlife programs on television, and was sure he had never heard David Attenborough or anyone else saying that squirrels liked doughnuts. He wondered whether they buried them.

First, of course, he had to find his squirrel. This proved more difficult than he had thought. He went to the farthest edges of the garden, pushed into the densest thickets. He gazed up into trees until his eyes ached.

"Squirrels! Come on, come on—nuts!"

He knew they were in there somewhere. But, like the bag lady, they just seemed to appear from nowhere.

"Squirrels! Puss, puss, puss—come on!"

He remembered something he had heard about the long hours crews had to wait for their subjects when filming in the wild. You didn't just go looking for leopards, for instance. You went to their haunts, then sat very still, and waited.

He decided to adopt this tactic. He chose a secluded area, shaded by high trees. There he opened his packet and scattered a few peanuts among the fallen leaves. They did not show up very well, but he hoped that his quarry would be able to sniff them out. He then concealed himself among the bushes, and waited.

For a while he kept his eyes on the nuts, from time to time twisting his head this way and that, scanning the trees above. Then he found his concentration slipping. He found himself remembering how sometimes he'd taken the other two to the park, to feed the ducks. He'd push Micky in his buggy, and Kev would run ahead, so he'd be forced to run as well, in case Kev got to the lake first and fell in. The buggy would rattle and leap, and Micky would wave his arms and chortle— and as often as not drop the bag, and all the food would go flying.

Then the three of them would stand at the water's edge and throw the bread, and it was as if they were kings. All the ducks and geese and moorhens would come sailing and flapping toward them, and they'd honk and quack and peck and squabble till all the bread was gone. That was the sad part, when all the birds would sail away, and you'd know it wasn't you they'd come for—it was just the food. Other people would come up and start feeding, and that was that. It was never the same watching other people throwing bread; you didn't have the same feeling.

They'd wander off then, and go on the swings and slides. Once Kev had fallen off and cut his head and had to go to the hospital for stitches, and everyone had wanted to know where their mother was. They'd said Josh was too young to be in charge of Micky and Kev, even after he'd tried to explain that it was all right, that Mum *let* them go. After that, a social worker had kept coming to the house.

He remembered the squirrels. His eyes moved back to the peanuts and encountered, with shock, a squirrel. It was all he could do not to cheer. He'd done it! He watched, enchanted, as it went, with little quick movements, to the bait. It was so close that he could see the separate hairs on its thick, curled tail, and hungered to touch it. But he knew that he must wait. Its eyes were black beads, rather like a bird's; its nose twitched. It was a jumpy, fidgety thing.

When it started nibbling a peanut, the feeling was a thousand times better than when the ducks gobbled the bread.

Stage one! he told himself exultantly. I'll stay absolutely still—I bet it can see me, really; I bet its eyes can see around corners, like birds'. So I'll come to this exact spot every day. It'll just accept me like one of the family. It might even come to me of its own accord— nibble my ear!

The prospect was delightful. And for the time being he was quite content to sit and watch and speculate whether this was a father squirrel, or a mother, or just a young one. He decided to comb the shops for a book about them. He wouldn't mind being a world expert on squirrels when he grew up. He'd keep them in his garden and they'd run in and out of the house and up the curtains and might even sleep on his bed.

He sat stock-still, watching and planning as the squirrel nibbled. Then it darted off, and ran effortlessly up a tree and was gone. Josh waited, in case it had gone to fetch its family. He felt he was becoming quite good at the waiting business.

I'm a world-class fidget. Miss Carpenter says so.

He waited what seemed a very long time, but the squirrel did not reappear. He came out from his hiding place and inspected the ground where the peanuts had been scattered and saw that they were all gone. Another wise thought came to him: Leave a few more—then it'll get used to coming and looking here. And so he did, and then set off down to the park to see which rides had the shortest lines.

Katy, alone in the bandstand, shut her eyes and conjured up a picture of her mother and felt her eyes fill. She wished the choice was not between staying here as slaves of the King and giving themselves up. She wished it were not a choice between Alton and Kirby House—or worse. She wished it were possible that she could go home.

She blinked away the tears and caught a blurry glimpse of silver. She had seen her first squirrel.

That's at home, she thought. It belongs here.

And when her eyes moved to the familiar dark shape of the bag lady, she found herself thinking, And her. She belongs.

She knew in her bones that the old woman was as much a part of Alton as the squirrels, and the calling cuckoos and ancient trees. By now she seemed almost one of the family, a reassuring presence after that awful encounter with the King. Brushing her eyes, Katy scrambled to her feet.

"Hello! Morning!"

She expected and received no answer. All she had in reply was a long look—a sad, soft look and a slow shaking of the head.

Katy had the curious feeling that the bag lady knew everything that had happened since their last meeting—could read her own thoughts, even.

"Do you live here?" she asked. "Do you belong?"

There was, of course, no answer.

"I'm always asking you questions, and you're never answering."

On the other hand, the old woman did meet Katy's eye. She did not merely go by, ignoring her.

"I expect there's a reason," Katy said. "I expect you're wondering what we're doing here. Me and Josh. That's his name. I'm Katy."

The old woman seemed to be waiting. She put down her bags. Katy went on.

"We've run away—not from our real homes, though. From this horrible children's home."

At least the bag lady listened, even if she did not speak.

"*We've* got bags—just the same as you. It was quite fun at first. But now . . . now . . . we don't feel safe anymore."

She heard her voice tremble, felt her eyes filling again.

The bag lady nodded. Then, amazingly, she beckoned—as if to say "Follow me"—picked up her bags, and went on. Katy, after the merest hesitation, followed. On the bag lady went, patiently trudging, lugging her bags. Once she turned, checking over her shoulder, and, seeing Katy, nodded and went on again.

Katy's eyes were fixed on the figure ahead and so she did not know where they were going until the bag lady stopped. Then, lifting her eyes, she saw they were by the stones again. They were at the very edge of that magic circle into which Katy had stepped unknowingly last night. Then, night had turned to day in the twinkling of an eye. Now, would day turn into night?

The bag lady turned and looked Katy full in the face. Her eyes seemed full of meaning, as if they were giving a message. Then she turned again, stepped in among the stones—and vanished.

Katy could not, absolutely not, believe it. She thought, for an instant, that she heard music, the dying shiver of a harp. From far away came the screams and laughter of the visitors, the daytime visitors.

"Where are you?" She spoke softly. Her eyes went fearfully up to the silently witnessing stones.

"Come back! Come back, won't you?"

She wondered then if the bag lady had meant her to follow, to go all the way after her.

"And if so—would *I* disappear?"

She was filled with terror at the thought of it, of vanishing, not being. Words and phrases crowded her head: *black hole—go in and never come out again—vanish!*

"No!" she screamed. "No!" And she ran.

EIGHT

Katy did not see Josh again till lunchtime. By then her stomach was hollow and noisy. She began to see what he meant about taking food. If you were starving, you had no choice.

And he gets hungrier than me, she thought. Hungrier than anyone. Got hollow legs.

She decided to stop lecturing him about stealing. In this place he was the only friend she had. And Alton was growing to be a dangerous place. Their being fugitives, hunted by the police, now seemed hardly to matter at all. The real danger lay in the King. Where was he now, she wondered? Where did he spend his days—and nights? She remembered Ollie's words. He was King of the castle. She raised her eyes to see the turrets of the Towers above the trees.

> I'm the king of the castle,
> And you're the dirty rascal!

She was that, all right, she thought. Later she would fetch her wash things and visit the tap in the orangery.

That'll make me feel better, she thought, as if she were her own mother talking to herself.

She had followed her nose toward the kiosks, and was keeping an eye open for abandoned food. What caught her eye was something quite different. A man was sitting reading a newspaper. There, on the front page, two familiar faces stared out: hers and Josh's.

She stopped dead, heart thudding. The headline was in heavy black type: HAVE YOU SEEN THESE KIDS?

It was unreal. Here she was, under the hot sun, and she was there, too, in a million newspapers—someone else, a self she hardly recognized. The man lowered the paper, briefly caught her eye, got up, and sauntered off.

Katy was elated. That man had just read the paper, seen her photo—and had not recognized her! She had been right: Alton Towers was the last place on earth they would think of looking for runaways. She longed to tell Josh, to share her triumph.

The gardens were the place where he would go, eventually. She had hardly started back there when she saw him. He was strolling past the Dome, eating chips from a paper cone.

"Josh!"

She ran to join him, then was snatching up chips because suddenly eating seemed more urgent than talking.

"Hey!"

"I'm ravenous!"

"Badgers don't eat chips!"

"*Or* foxes!" she said with her mouth full.

They emptied the cone, the earlier quarrel forgotten.

"Listen—you'll never believe!"

She told him first about the newspaper. The bag lady could wait. It was going to be hard to find words to tell about her.

"Front *page*? I'm a star!" He flung out his arms and struck a pose.

"They weren't very good photos. Couldn't've been—he hardly even noticed me!"

"Front page! Fame!"

"Not really," said Katy. He was not taking her news as she had expected.

"'Tis! Only famous people get put on the front page!"

"And murderers," she said.

"Here—have one of these!"

He dug into the bag and fetched out a sticky bun, and she gratefully wolfed it with not a thought, let alone word, about stealing.

"Listen!" It was his turn for news now. "I've been talking to Ollie."

"Him!"

"No—he's not so bad, really. He says the King was here first, before him. He got him same as Ollie got us!"

"Serve him right!"

"And he says the King needs us—and him."

"What d'you mean, needs?"

"The way he looks! Sticks out a mile!"

"Telling me—him and his horrible hair!"

"If he was to go around like we do, they'd spot him—bound to. Recognize him."

"So why doesn't he shave it all off and go around bald?" She laughed.

"Don't be daft," he told her. "Anyway, he stays in hiding, see, and Ollie goes out and does all the nicking."

"And us, now. He *is* like Fagin."

"No skin off my nose!" He pranced ahead. "Easy! Easy as pie!"

Katy hurried after him. "Josh—I want to show you something."

It was easier to demonstrate what happened than tell it in words. It made more believable something she hardly believed herself.

Once at the stones, she started believing it again. She stood for a moment, feeling something alien in the air. It reminded her of how, when she was little, her sack from Santa Claus had always been left in the living room. She would wake early, and tiptoe down through the dark, silent house. When she pushed open the door, there was the living room, familiar as ever, yet somehow strange, altered. The very furniture stood stiff and foreign. It had witnessed that secret visit. The air was filled with a powerful presence. Once, she had bolted back upstairs, jumped into bed, and pulled the covers right over her head, heart pounding.

So, now, she felt the air printed with vanished presences. She hesitated to set foot there.

"Go on then—what?" Josh's voice broke through.

"It—she—I was following her. She looked over her shoulder, to make sure I was there."

"Go *on,* then!"

"And—she stepped forward—like this"—now she

did step into the different air, the ring of power—"and vanished!"

"What?"

"She did!"

"Dream on!"

"She *did*. Listen, will you? You don't listen!"

Josh marched right in among the stones. He cocked his head this way and that, like a bird.

"Vanished! Old men with harps! You going barmy, or what? Hey—am *I* invisible?" He peered closely at his own hands. "Don't seem to be. Not ezackly."

Katy stamped her foot. "*You* saw the lights; *you* heard the music!"

"Might've," he admitted.

"You did—you know you did!"

"All right—did."

"Well, then!"

"Well, what?" he said. "That Old Mother Alton, she never even *says* anything!"

"Not in words, but—what did you call her?"

"Old Mother Alton."

"Well," said Katy, "I wouldn't be surprised if she *was*."

That night it rained. Katy woke up in the darkness to the cold and wet. The rain was spattering heavily about her, and she felt her clothes already wet.

"Oh, no!" She shivered. Can't stop here, she thought. Catch our deaths.

She shook Josh, who lay curled, still sleeping. He stirred and muttered.

"Josh! Wake up!"

"What—? Oh, no—'s raining!"

"It's pouring. C'mon; we'll have to find somewhere dry."

They scrambled to their feet and pushed their way through the dripping leaves. Above them the floodlit orangery flashed and shimmered, adrift.

"In there!" Josh whispered. "Safe as houses, Ollie says!"

The rain was coming down in sheets. Already they were soaked. They ran, their eyes fixed on the lights.

"No! Look!" Katy stopped, and pulled at Josh's sleeve.

"Come *on*! I'm soaked!"

"No! Look!" She pointed.

Through the streaming glass of the orangery they saw a figure, unmistakable with its high cock's comb.

"'S him!"

"The King!"

He was pacing—up, down, steadily like a caged lion.

"Where's Ollie?" whispered Josh.

The figure paced and turned, paced and turned. The cock's comb was turned into a crown by the watery glass. Had he been there since dark, sleepless and prowling?

"What's he *doing*?"

"Dunno. Get spotted, though, if he doesn't watch it!"

"Come on," said Katy. "That Refuge place."

It was unthinkable now that they should shelter in the orangery, share it with the King. By the time they reached the Refuge they were drenched. It was cold in there, and smelled of wet stone and ferns. By day, in the sunshine, it had looked a snug enough place. They groped their way into the darkness, and were at least no longer in the rain. They were crouched, shivering.

"M-my t-t-teeth are chattering!" Josh said.

"We'll *never* sleep in here. Listen—what was he *doing* in there?"

"D-dunno. T-t-trying to keep warm."

"No. It was spooky. *He's* spooky."

They sat shivering, picturing that solitary, pacing figure. They looked out into the dark and wet. All about them the gardens were alive with the ticking of rain.

"F-fox in a den now, all right," said Josh.

"F-foxes don't catch pneumonia!" Katy's own teeth were chattering now. "And they've got fur!"

The long, wet, sleepless night lay ahead of them.

"Can't ezackly play I Spy," came Josh's voice suddenly, and they both laughed, silly, frightened laughs, because the weather had turned against them. It made all the difference.

"If it keeps on raining—for days, I mean—we'll have to give up," Katy said.

"Nah! We'll find somewhere dry. Soon as it's light, tomorrow."

"We'll d-die!" said Katy, and meant it. In the world outside, if you were cold and wet you went inside. You had a hot bath, changed your clothes. In the world outside the weather didn't matter. Here, they were at its mercy.

They did not know how long they sat, shivering and afraid, before they heard the harp. Its notes threaded the steadily falling rain as if they were both written into the same score.

"Listen!"

They scrambled to the mouth of the tiny cave, and sure enough, there were the lights, the sparks pulled to candle flames by the prism of the rain. They gazed for a moment and then, wordlessly, went out again into the wetness and made toward the lights.

When they reached the stones they both saw the snow white head, the golden harp in the storm of light. They did not stop, but walked steadily forward until the moment came when they were out of the dark and rain.

They stepped into broad day, and were not surprised. The music rippled to silence. The old man raised his head. They were not afraid, but were in awe of him. Katy felt that she must say something, but was tongue-tied, never having been in the presence of magic before.

"Who are you, please?" was all she managed at last.

"I am Quantum," he replied.

"Please, sir"—it was Josh now—"where are we?"

The old man smiled. "You are where it is safe."

"It's just—it's just that it's dark out there, and wet."

"Not now. Go—see for yourselves."

"You mean—you mean back in the gardens?"

"Is it light out there—like here?"

"Perhaps . . . you need to sleep, I think. Perhaps it

should be dark . . . dark, but dry and warm. . . ." He ran his fingers over the strings. "There. . . ." He turned back to the children. "Now you may go."

Josh turned, but Katy held her ground. "Excuse me," she said timidly.

He waited courteously.

"Please, sir, today—yesterday—there was this old woman, you see, and I saw her—"

The old man was holding up his hand. "Do not ask that question. Not now."

"Oh! Oh—sorry!" Katy stammered. "I didn't mean to—"

She turned to follow Josh, who waited by the edge of the stones. They stared at each other, dizzy with disbelief.

"Dark but dry," Josh muttered. "I don't believe it. Still—here goes! Ready?"

Katy nodded.

They took deep breaths and walked away. At some particular point, as they took one particular step, day turned to night.

"'S true!"

"Oh, it's warm!"

An owl hooted. The moon came out from behind a cloud and bathed the valley in its chill light. They stood and looked about them, rapt and silent. And as they gazed they became aware, slowly, that they were in another place. They knew this not because of things that were there, but because of things that were not there.

They were in a wooded valley, and it might have

been the same valley. But it might have been that valley when time began. There was not a single sign that humans had ever set foot there. Gone were the bandstand and pagoda, the orangery and the soaring cables of the Skyride. They turned their eyes fearfully and saw that even the towers and turrets of the great house had vanished.

They stood and gazed, and had not the least idea that, again, they were being watched.

"It's all gone!" Josh's voice came in a whisper. "Orangery 'n' all!"

"But it's the same place!" Katy whispered back. "Must be!"

"We're not . . . not in a black hole, are we? Time going backward . . . ?"

Katy did not know. Again an owl hooted. She yawned.

"Oh, I'm tired. . . ."

"Same here. Let's find somewhere to sleep."

They walked on through the altered gardens and found a patch of turf shaded from the moon by overhanging branches.

The watcher followed them, step by step.

Wordlessly they lay down, curling themselves for sleep.

"Night, Mr. Fox!" Katy whispered, but Josh's eyes were already closed. She shut her own.

The other figure under the moon stood and waited. Faint and faraway came the sound of children's laughter, as if school were out. The pair breathed deeply, gently. Josh's thumb fell away from his mouth.

The watcher stepped forward then, and gazed down at them. She stood for a time, and then drew something from a pocket, stooped, and placed it carefully by Katy's curled hand.

She stood back, and then the moon went behind a cloud.

NINE

Katy was the first to wake. She knew at once that it was dawn by the light and the birds. She shivered, feeling her clothes damp against her skin.

"It was raining. We—oh, whatever . . . ?"

She sat stiffly up and saw that they had been sleeping not in a hidey-hole, but right across a path that led to a wooden bridge. She gasped, and shook Josh—hard. He muttered his way out of sleep and blinked his eyes.

"Quick! Look where we are!"

They were in full view, where the security guards and dogs could have stepped right over them. Then she remembered. She could see in her mind's eye the moonlit turf, the overhanging branches. She stared down at the asphalt and saw something lying there, right by her.

"Whatever . . . ?"

She picked it up. It looked like a gingerbread man with its starfish arms and legs. Carved from wood, worn and old, with eyes, nose, mouth. "A doll!"

It stared up at her, blank and mute.

"Not a proper one."

"But how did it—"

"Spooky. . . ."

She jerked her eyes away from that wooden gaze.

"Come on—back to the den!"

Katy snatched up the doll, and they went back there and pushed through the dripping leaves and found their hidey-hole and all their things sodden. What had seemed so snug and sheltered was now damp underfoot, water still spattering from the trees above. The pair stood forlornly, taking it in.

"Home sweet home!" said Katy, and giggled because she was genuinely frightened, and trying to hide it.

"Blinking mud bath!"

"The things inside the bags'll be all right," Katy said, being sensible, being mother.

"But *we're* still wet. Last night . . ."

They stared at each other. What had happened seemed impossible now, unimaginable.

"It happened," said Katy firmly. "It really happened. To both of us." She was glad of that.

"I expect we must have dried a bit when we were asleep. It was warm—"

"And dry—just like he said."

They were mystified. Josh shivered.

"Think I'll go in the orangery. Dry in there. Get some more sleep."

Katy was surprised. "Aren't you going to the kiosks? We've got to get stuff for the King. And what about our breakfast?"

"Not hungry."

Now she was alarmed. In all the time she had

known Josh, he had never missed a meal. Usually, he managed two meals for the price of one.

"Don't you feel well?"

"Not ezackly. Jus' cold."

"It'll be your wet things," Katy said, being sensible again. "Take your bag up with you and change into something dry."

She went up there with him. While he pulled off his wet T-shirt she splashed her face and hands at the tap.

"I'm thirsty."

"Here—give us your bottle. I'll fill it."

He arranged himself for sleep, and she put the filled bottle by him.

"I s'pose . . . I s'pose I'd better go to the kiosks."

"Up to you," he murmured, eyes already closed.

"Even if you're not hungry, I'd better get some stuff. For . . . for the King."

He did not reply.

"I'll go, then." She sounded braver than she felt. "Then I'll wake you up when I get back. You can't stay here long—they'll find you."

She fished among his things and found the plastic carrier.

"See you, then."

"See you. . . ," he said very faintly.

She went out into the cool gardens. She raised her eyes and saw the turrets of the Towers, drew a deep breath, and began to march toward them. She realized now how much braver Josh was than she. He went willingly out of the safety of the gardens to scavenge, to find the things they needed to survive.

And he's younger than me, she thought, and was a little ashamed. Then, I could never have done this without him.

At home, for ages it had been she who had gone out and shopped, posted letters. It was she who had washed and cleaned and done all the necessary things. Her mother had relied on her. Now, it was she who relied on Josh.

She was scared. She knew that all she had to do was pick through the plastic bags behind the kiosks. It was not even stealing. All the stuff had been thrown out. But the security men could be about. And then there were Ollie and the King.

You've got to be brave, she told herself. Everybody has.

She marched on, and that was when she saw it: that dark, torn shape flap-flapping down among the trees.

"'S that again!"

She shaded her eyes and watched it go, beating noiselessly down, then out of sight. Even now, alone as she was, she was not afraid. She was simply mystified. There was a secret, invisible pattern in the valley, and somewhere that dark shape fitted in.

Cautiously she crossed the wide path by the Towers, and plunged into the shrubbery beyond. She looked only left and right. She did not look up to the house itself, and so did not know that she was being watched.

By now she was used to weaving her way through bushes. These were still wet from the night's rain, and gave off powerful smells. She was getting used to that, too. She had not known that green things all have their own particular scent.

Then she heard something that made her stop and stiffen. It was a human sound. It was the sound of sobbing.

For a moment she was tempted to turn and run. Her only friend at Alton was Josh, and he was up in the orangery, sleeping. Whoever this was had nothing to do with her. The very sound of weeping filled her with dread. Her mother had cried, all the time, sometimes noisily, sometimes softly and hopelessly. There was nothing you could do about it.

And yet she was curious. It was still not long past dawn. Who could be out here already, and weeping? She went on carefully, very carefully, peering ahead, until she saw a figure hunched on the ground, hugging his knees, head buried.

"Ollie!" She gasped the word aloud without meaning to. He did not hear her. She stood watching, disbelieving, then went forward. Timidly she touched his shaking shoulder.

He jumped as if stung, saw her, and a sleeve went swiftly over his wet eyes.

"Don't cry."

"I ain't! What're you doing sneaking around?"

"I—I've come to get food. Instead of Josh."

"You'd better! Go on, then—get it!"

Still she hung back. Ollie hugging his knees, Ollie with wet eyes, was a different person from the one she hated. She remembered what Josh had told her, about the King having power over him as well as themselves.

"Don't cry," she heard herself say again. "It'll be all right."

He stared at her. "What do you know about anything?"

"Not much," she admitted. "But when you've had a cry, you'll feel better."

"I told you. I ain't crying."

"Why haven't *you* got a home?" she asked.

His face screwed in misery. He did not look at her. "I ain't, that's all. I know one thing. Wish I'd stayed in London; wish I'd never come here."

"Because of—the King?"

He nodded, still not looking at her.

"Why don't you just go, then? Leave him."

"You don't know anything about it."

"The police aren't after you—you said so yourself."

"Look, drop it, will you? None of your business."

"Sorry."

He did look at her then. "Look, if you kids've got any sense, you'll clear out while there's still time."

She waited.

"You don't know what he's like. He ain't . . . ain't human."

She had a picture of the King last night, pacing up and down, up and down behind the watery glass.

"But we'll be caught if we do, and sent away somewhere. Worse even than Kirby."

He looked at her then, properly, for the first time.

"Poor kids," he said, almost to himself. Then, "Had a sister your age. Katy."

"My name!"

"Yeah . . . well . . . not seen her for years. Split us up, see."

"Like Josh!"

"What?"

"He's got two brothers—little ones. They split them up. It's horrible."

"Yeah. Well. It is horrible."

He was gazing into nowhere again, his face bleak.

"Quite a cozy little chat!" said a soft voice. They both whirled around.

He was there, the King, arms folded, looking down at them. He might have been there for a long time, listening.

"I—I was just going for the food," Katy stammered.

"You!" He was addressing Ollie.

"Yes—yes, chief!" Ollie sprang to his feet.

"Your mouth's too big," the King told him.

"Yes, chief."

"Say it."

"My—my mouth's too big."

He turned his gaze on Katy. "Where's the other one?" he asked.

"He—he's asleep. We got wet last night."

"Find somewhere dry, did you?"

"Yes. No. Sort of."

"Where was that, I wonder . . . ?" He eyed her narrowly. "Not many dry places. . . ."

"It wasn't all that dry," Katy said. She knew that, whatever happened, she must not say a word about the lights and music, the ring of power among the stones.

"I wonder. . . ." he said softly. Then, "Like it here, do you?"

"Y-yes. Yes."

"Course you do. Why wouldn't you? But if you want to stay, you obey the rules. Right, Ollie?"

"Yeah. Yeah, chief!"

"And the first rule is that I am king."

"Sure, we know that, chief," said Ollie eagerly. "You've been—"

"Shut—up!" He was looking at Katy.

"Say it. Say 'You're king.'"

She could not, could not for the life of her. If anyone was king at Alton, it was that man who could turn night to day at the touch of a string, and sat at the center of an endless eruption of lights.

"Say it."

She stared down at the ground to avoid that hard white face.

"Perhaps if we twist your arm," said the King softly. "Ollie!"

Ollie stepped forward, grabbed Katy, and pinned her arms behind her.

"Stop! You're hurting!"

There came the bark of a dog, quite close by. They froze, all three of them. There came more barking, men's voices.

"Run for it!"

The King was gone, Ollie after him. Katy was terrified. She turned and ran back the way she had come, back toward the garden. She ran blindly, straight into the bag lady. She felt arms go around her, the thick folds of a cloak.

Then the men were there, and the dog.

"What's with him?" one of them said.

Katy heard the soft growling, right by her. She squeezed her eyes tight shut.

"Search me. Look at that—fur on end!"

"Ghosts!" A man's laugh. "In broad day. Here, Prince; here boy!"

She heard the panting of the dog, its paws treading softly. She could not see it, she could not see anything, buried as she was in the folds of the cloak. But—*why did they not see her?*

The footsteps retreated, the voices faded. Slowly Katy slipped back, out of the sheltering cloak, blinking in the light. She stared up at the calm face of the bag lady, trying to take in what had happened.

"Invisible!" she gasped at last. "We were invisible!"

In their room the security men were coming off duty, taking off their wet things.

One of the day shift had already arrived. "Rained a bucketful last night," he said. "Rather you than me. Is it forecast again?"

He switched on the television. "Those kids still missing, then. Makes you wonder what *they* did last night."

". . . has left the hospital. Later today she is expected to appear at a press conference and appeal for Katy's safe return. The mother of Joshua Grey has now been traced. She went to Stoke police station after seeing reports of her son's disappearance in the press. She is reported to be very distressed, and is under sedation. The police are appealing to everyone in the area to make a thorough check of their premises, particularly outbuildings and sheds."

"Missed the weather, by the look of it." He switched the set off.

"Make sure you check the outbuildings and sheds, Bill," said Dave, grinning. "Oh—and watch Prince."

"Why's that?"

"Hallucinations. Seeing things."

"Oh, yes? Had one of his little turns, has he? Where—Her Ladyship's Garden?"

"No—funny thing that, wasn't it, George? Not far off the house. Never done it there before."

"The works," George said. "Fur on end, growling—and not a blind thing in sight."

"Ghosts *aren't* in sight," Bill said.

"Ah, but we're talking daylight here—broad daylight."

"You *what*?"

"Less than an hour ago."

Bill laughed. "Dog must be heading for a nervous breakdown. Any ghost around here in the daytime's strictly for the Haunted House. Anyone seen my cap?"

TEN

"I'm not going back there! I'm not!"

Josh, newly woken, had hardly taken in her story.

"I daren't!"

"'S all right, Katy," he murmured. "Not hungry."

"He said—he said, 'If you kids've got any sense, you'll get out while there's still time!'"

She could not seem to get through to him.

"Be all right. . . ." He closed his eyes again.

"Josh! You can't go back to sleep! We'll have to move."

He huddled the more, curled like a hedgehog.

"*Josh!*" She tugged at the sweater that pillowed his head.

"Ouch—ouch—my head!" He struggled upright and shivered. "Brr! Cold!"

"You must've caught cold. Last night. You'll soon feel better. Oh, please, Josh!"

He got shakily to his feet, and Katy helped him pick up his things.

"We'll take these back to the den. There's nowhere else."

"Ugh—it'll still be soaking in there!" He followed her out of the warm, dry orangery, still protesting.

They were spattered with water as they pushed their way back into the den. Josh stared down at what had been his bed.

"Couldn't I just go to the bandstand?" he pleaded.

"No, you can't. Anyone could see you. Our photos were in the paper, remember."

"That man didn't recognize you."

"No, and if we act normal, no one *will* recognize us."

"Badger, badger, badger! *Am* acting normal," Josh said, wrapping his arms around himself. He was shivering again.

"You want to keep your voices down!"

They both jumped.

"Hear you out there, you know," said Ollie, pale face framed by leaves. "Got a lot to learn, you two."

"We—we don't know if we want to," said Katy. "Not anymore."

"Y-yes we do," said Josh weakly.

"Dog give you a fright, did it? What did you do— climb a tree?"

"Why are you being so horrible again?" Katy asked, partly to avoid the question. "That King's got you right under his thumb!"

Ollie looked disconcerted, shamefaced almost. "Ah, well . . . we're all in this together."

"You're t-telling me," Josh said.

"Except *him,*" Katy said. "Couldn't you—couldn't you just leave him, and come in with us?"

"What—be in your gang?" Ollie was scornful. "We're not playing games here."

"But—couldn't you?"

"No. You can't do the King down and get away with it."

"But we'd be three to one! What could he do? He's only human."

"Is he?" said Ollie.

They stared at him. He was serious. Katy thought of the bag lady, the harpist. They looked human, but were certainly something more.

"There's more than you know going on around here."

Did Ollie and the King know of the invisible pattern woven into the valley?

"There's certainly more than four of us living here," said Katy, trying to test him.

"What d'you mean?" His face was alert, suspicious.

She drew a deep breath. "The bag lady."

Silence, but for the drip, drip of wet leaves.

"The *what*?"

He had not seen her. Katy wished she had not spoken.

"Oh—nothing."

"Come on—the what? *Bag* lady?"

"I just—just thought I saw one. Couldn't've, though. That's what I thought. Why would an old woman come here?" She spoke fast; perhaps too fast. Ollie was still eyeing her suspiciously. She gabbled on. "Bet *your* granny wouldn't go on the Thunder Looper; bet *she* wouldn't go on the—"

"I haven't got a granny. And if you know something, you'd better tell me."

"We don't!"

He eyed her. "Kids . . . ," he murmured. "Just don't try anything, that's all. The King's got his eye on you. Got plans for you."

"What . . . sort of plans?"

He shrugged. "Dunno. All I know is, he's been waiting for a kid to turn up. Been saying it ever since I come here. Some plan he's got. Over the moon he was, when you two turned up."

"He doesn't need us to nick food. You can do it."

"Course I can," he agreed. "Easy. Just getting you trained, that's all. First, you nick food, then . . ." He paused. "Then he's got some other little jobs for you. Soon, I shouldn't wonder."

There was a quick shiver of leaves, and he was gone.

"What—what did he mean, little jobs?"

"I'm freezing," Josh said.

"You don't think they know about—about—?"

"Oops! Nearly forgot!"

They jumped again as Ollie's face reappeared.

"Food! Better jump to it—don't want to upset the King, do we?"

They both went to the kiosks. Katy felt a little ashamed. Josh was not well. But she dared not go by herself, with the memory of that recent pursuit, of that softly growling dog. This time there might be no bag lady to save her. Even the fact that she *had* been saved was in itself frightening. She had been invisible. For that short time while the dog sniffed and snarled and circled, she had not existed, had become thin air.

They took a bag each, remembering how Ollie had snatched everything the previous day. Josh was not hungry now, but his old squirrel's instinct was still there. He had always felt the need to provision himself against an uncertain future. Now the future was uncertain as never before.

He did not want to go. "I ache all over."

"Thought you were Mr. Fox. *Foxes* don't catch colds."

"And *badgers* are always badgering. Badger, badger, badger!" He trailed after her, muttering.

They hurried from bin to bin, kiosk to kiosk, snatching up doughnuts, pizzas, potatoes—even a few pieces of cold, battered fish. They also had an unexpected piece of luck.

"Look!" Katy pointed. There, lying by the door to one of the kiosks, was a shining black square. She picked it up, and it turned out to be two unused garbage bags, evidently dropped.

"Ground sheets!" she said. "Keep us dry!"

She pushed them not into the bag, but down the front of her jacket. Ollie might be capable of taking both bags.

She had hardly done so when they heard the vans and trucks that meant the day at Alton Towers had begun in earnest. They set off back to the gardens.

"'Spect *he'll* jump out at us any minute," said Josh, meaning Ollie.

"If only they weren't here—him and the King. It'd be all right without them."

It was true. They had begun to settle, worked out a routine that could go on for days, weeks, months. Even the weather could surely be managed, in the end.

Ollie waylaid them in the gardens. "Nice work, kids!" He took one of the bags. "The King wants to see you, later."

They did not reply.

"Told you it wouldn't be long. Got one or two jobs for you—*real* jobs."

"Well, I'm not doing them!" Katy said.

"Oh, I think you'd better. Doesn't do to upset the King."

"You might be frightened of him. I'm not."

"Ah, but what about this?"

He dug into his jeans and fished out the crumpled note.

"I—we don't care, not anymore. Josh is poorly."

"I'm not—not really."

"You are, then! And we're sick of always hiding and getting wet and eating cold doughnuts!"

Ollie was clearly disconcerted. "You're never giving yourselves up!"

"We might."

"*I* shan't," Josh said.

"Well, *I* might."

"You're mad," said Ollie. "I told you—they'll send you away somewhere."

"Don't care!"

He looked worried now, confused. The tables had been turned. There was something else in his eyes, too. Fear.

"Look," he said, "don't."

"You told us yourself to get out!"

"Yes, but—but—"

"But what?"

"If you go, then it's just . . . me and him again."

"Shut up, Katy," Josh said. "We aren't going."

"And he'll blame me. And we'll have to start all over again."

"Start what?"

He hesitated for a moment. "Looking. Looking for a kid."

"A kid? He's mad," said Katy. "And you're mad, sticking with him. Come on, Josh!"

She set off, and heard Ollie's voice come after her. "No! Wait! Don't do it! I warn you!"

Josh caught up with her. "What did you do that for? Katy—you won't really give up, will you?"

"I don't know. But I know one thing. I'm not doing anything for the King."

"Might only be something little. No harm in it. Oh, don't, Katy, please don't!"

She looked at him sideways and saw that he was close to tears. Usually there were only tears when he was in a rage.

"You're not well," she said.

"I'm all right."

"We'll put those liners down when we get back, and you can lie down."

This was what they did. Back in the den, Josh curled up without protest.

"You'll feel better when you wake up," Katy told him.

"What'll you do?"

"I'll think of something."

He was already asleep when she left the den. It was only just past eight. She was alone but for the birds and the odd streaking squirrel. She could not come out of hiding till nine, when the first visitors would arrive. She really did not know what to do.

She wandered up to the Refuge, and checked that her ten-pound note was still there, looking carefully about her first. It was, and after a moment's hesitation, she took it out and pushed it into the back pocket of her jeans.

I'll buy a book when the shops open, she told herself. A book was a way of escaping from yourself and your surroundings, and she was beginning to feel the need for escape. She marveled again at how differently things had turned out from the way she had imagined. She had thought that life at Alton would be a nonstop pleasure ride, with all the fun of camping thrown in. Nothing had prepared her for what they had found, for the bag lady, and the powerhouse of the stones, for Ollie and the King. Nothing had prepared her for the mystery.

When she had told Ollie that she was ready to give up, she had partly meant it, and was partly calling his bluff. She was torn between fear of what lay in store in the outside world, and fear of being in the power of the King. Beyond that lay the mystery, and she was reluctant to leave it unsolved. The pull of that was stronger than anything. It seemed to demand something of her.

She looked at her watch and tried to conjure up the scene at Kirby House. They would be having breakfast in that dark, echoing room. The packed lunches would be lying ready on the trestle table at the far end. She was glad not to be there. Then she pictured her own house, and saw her mother, smiling, as she had in the old days. She would be glad to be there again, for the last few months to be wiped out as if they had never been.

Without even realizing it, as if drawn, she had come to the stones. They stood silent, rooted and contained. What did they know? she wondered, and wished they had tongues to tell. She went over and clasped one, as she had on that first day, and now, as then, was unaware of a watcher.

Again she felt the unutterable hardness, the strength of the thing. It was icy against hand and cheek, and she smelled its clean stone smell. Perhaps she half hoped this act would trigger something, set in motion some kind of friendly magic.

What she saw, when she finally stepped back, was the King. He stood watching her with a curious intentness as if he, too, were waiting for something to happen.

"Oh!" She looked swiftly about. "I didn't—where's Ollie?"

"Like it here, don't you?" he said. "I wonder why. . . ."

"I—I don't! Not particularly."

"Oh, yes," he said. "I think so."

She stared back at him, half mesmerized. She was alone with him, and began now to understand Ollie's fear.

"Tell me," he said coaxingly.

"Tell you . . . what?"

"Oh, I think you know," he said. "Thing's you've seen, heard."

"I—I don't know what you mean."

"Come on; you can tell me. No harm. You're a kid, aren't you? And kids see things, hear things. . . ."

She said nothing. She was frozen.

"Might even have a little reward for you. Come on . . . tell . . . tell. . . ."

He had been advancing on her, and was now right close. His eyes held hers, against her will. Still she said nothing.

"I shall find out, in the end," he said. He waited. "Where's your mum, then?"

She was thrown by the sudden change of tack. "In hospital."

"Ah. . . . And your dad?"

"I haven't got one."

"Brothers, sisters?"

She shook her head dumbly. Her eyes ached under the force of his gaze.

"What a shame," he said softly. "All alone . . ."

She found her voice. "I'm not, then! I've got Mum!"

He smiled with unchanging eyes. "But you're not

with your mum. In a home, ain't you? What if she stays in the hospital? What if she never comes out? What if—"

"No!" she screamed, and clapped her hands over her ears. "I'm not listening; I'm not! No!"

And with the scream she found the power to look away from that cruel face, and to run. She ran from him and thought that she was leaving him behind, with the stones, and did not expect the hand on her shoulder, and screamed again.

He was panting, his face contorted. He gripped and shook her. "Listen, you, you can forget it! Give yourself up! You'd better not! You know where Ollie is, this very moment? Do you?"

She shook her head.

"He's doing a break-in."

She stared back at him, not understanding.

"A big one." He smiled. "Keep leaving your things lying about, don't you? But *we* know where they are, me and Ollie. What if something's missing?"

He was triumphant now, and still she did not know why.

"And what if . . . what if something's been dropped? What if you were ever so careless, and dropped it at the scene of the crime?"

Now she understood, and was flooded with shock and horror.

"The pigs won't know whose it is. Not if you lie low. But you give yourself up, and—"

"No! You can't've!"

"Can't I? Better get back and check your things, hadn't you?"

He gave her a final violent shake. "I'm king here!" he said.

ELEVEN

The image that burned in Katy's head as she made for the den was of the wooden doll. It was only hours since she had found it on the path by the bridge, but already it seemed light-years ago. She had stuffed it deep in her bag, unwilling to meet its blank gaze, to explain to herself how it had come there.

Now she knew that it was the only thing that mattered. It was the link between herself and that other Alton, the Alton of different times and weathers, the one that sprang out of the endlessly born lights.

Was that the thing Ollie had stolen, to plant at the scene of the break-in? If so, then it would not matter, in a way. The doll was *not* hers; no one could possibly link it to her. Yet she wanted above all for that carved figure still to be there.

In the den she dropped to her knees and pulled the things out of her bag. T-shirts, sweatshirts, sneakers, toilet bag—ah! The doll was there. She sat back on her heels, gazing at it, trying to wrench some kind of meaning out of it.

I'll keep it with me from now on, she thought. It would not quite fit into her jeans pocket, but the pockets of her jacket were deep and wide. She thrust it in, then turned back to the heap of belongings.

It was the flashlight that was missing. It was just an ordinary Woolworth flashlight like thousands of others. But at Kirby House she had kept it on her nightstand, to read by after the others had gone to sleep. And it'll have my fingerprints on it!

So what the King had said was true. As long as she lay low, no one could possibly connect it with her. But if she gave herself up . . .

Her eye fell on Josh's bag. She guessed that something would be missing from that, too. Only he could tell what. He lay, enviably absent, for the time being out of the world's reach. She was half tempted to wake him, to tell him about the break-in, the King's threats.

There was no point. Nothing could undo it. Slowly she pushed her things back into her bag. Because she felt the need to do something—anything—she left the den and began to make her way back to the stones. It would be later, much later in the day before any outside visitors went there. As she approached, she looked warily about her for any sign of the King. He, too, seemed drawn to the stones.

At the edge of the ring she stopped. Some instinct told her that merely to step casually in was not enough. A ritual of some kind was needed. She drew the wooden figure from her pocket. It was warm now, faintly alive. She held it in both hands and raised it awkwardly, as if in offering. There should be words, too. Some kind of incantation would be best, but she could not think of the right words. She knew only that she and Josh were in terrible danger and needed help. What she said, softly, was the one word *please,* then stepped forward.

She stepped forward, and at the same time shut her eyes, as though that would help the working of magic. In that moment she thought she heard a shiver of harp strings. Still clasping the doll, she drew a deep breath, and opened her eyes.

She was still there, in among the towering stones, and it was still day, but she knew at once that she was out of the world she had left, because of the great silence and because of the child.

The pair stood, eyes locked. That other child was skinny and fair and dressed in bluish gray rags. Her eyes were stretched wide, because a charm had worked for her, too, when she had placed her doll by the sleeping Katy. Her eyes moved to the carved figure.

"Mine!" she said.

"You?" Katy had not known where the doll had come from, had hardly dared think, but somewhere at the back of her mind had been a picture of the bag lady.

"It worked," the child said.

"How?"

"It's mine, and you brought it." She held out her hand, and Katy gave it to her.

"I'm Katy."

"Beth."

"Where are we?" Katy asked. "Whose time, I mean?"

"I did come here long ago," Beth said. "What trouble are you in?"

"Trouble? How do you know?"

The girl laughed. "She brought you here, didn't she?"

"Who?"

"Why, Old Mother Alton, of course! She brung us all here!"

"But—"

"Old Mother Hen, we do call her! Like a hen with chicks she be, cluckin' and shakin' her wings!"

She meant the bag lady. And at the mention of wings, Katy remembered the dark flapping shape that had tumbled out of the sky that first day, long ago— was it only a week?

"Yes," Katy said. "She brought us here."

"And shall you stay?" asked the child eagerly.

"Stay?"

"Oh, you can choose," said Beth. "All of us here— we chose it!"

"I don't get it," Katy said.

"'Tis easy! You choose to stay, and the king, he makes your song, and—"

"*Who?*"

"The king."

Katy was stunned. "But—he's terrible! I hate him!"

"Oh, no," said Beth softly. "Oh, *no*! Lovely 'e be, him and his music."

"Beth, hey! I've found the—" The voice broke off. Katy turned and saw a boy around her own age. He was wearing jeans and a T-shirt. She could not take it in. She had thought herself back in time.

"Hi!" he said. "You just come?"

"She hasn't chosen yet," Beth told him. "Matthew, this be."

He grinned. "Matt. It's great here—choose it!"

"Listen," Katy said, "you said the king—him with the harp, you mean?"

"Course!" the boy said. "Quantum—that's his name. He makes your song."

"But . . . out there . . . there's someone else calls himself the King!"

The pair exchanged uneasy glances.

"She means the Enemy," the boy said.

"After the harp!" Beth looked frightened now.

"What's he like?" the boy asked.

"Horrible. Tall, with a white face and punk hair. But why's he after the harp?"

"Look," Matt said, "that music makes the world happen. You've heard it? You've seen those lights?"

Katy nodded.

"They come out of nowhere. Bet you thought they were like 'Top of the Pops' on TV."

"I didn't, actually," Katy told him.

"Well, they're not. *He* makes them happen—Quantum. He can make anything happen—anything!"

Katy stared, first at one, then at the other, intent and unsmiling.

"The Enemy," Matt said. "You told him anything?"

"No. But . . . he's got power over us. Me and Josh—there's two of us."

"Dare you fight him?" Matt asked. "You must! We can't! The harp!"

When Katy walked out of the ring of stones, she was still clutching the wooden doll. Beth had given it back to her; it was her passport back into that other Alton.

"At night, you can always come," Matt had said. "You knew that?"

Katy had nodded.

"Just keep that safe. If the Enemy gets hold of it . . ."

Now, passing the orangery, Katy thrust the wooden figure back into the pocket of her jacket. Though I can't keep it on all day, she thought. Looks as if it might get hot.

The sun was already out, flashing on every leaf and twig in the drenched valley. If she half closed her eyes, the light went into rays and spokes.

In the den Josh was still sleeping in his cocoon of leaves. By him was the bag of food. She sat on a garbage bag, took out a baked potato, and bit into it, trying to imagine it was hot. Someone had told her once that if you yourself were very hot, you could cool down simply by telling yourself that you were cold. She had not really believed this. Now, the potato certainly had not warmed up by her wishing.

The sun was shafting through the trees and lit a cobweb, perilously strung between boughs, where a spider was still at work. She was surprised by the thought that all day long, as people plundered the park in search of fun, that spider was steadily and secretly spinning, and so, no doubt, were thousands of others like it. It rose and fell, deft and intent, and she marveled that it should make a cobweb so perfect and intricate. It had not learned the art; it had come into the world knowing it. That in itself was astounding.

It's been programmed. Have spiders got microchips instead of brains? And if so, where? They haven't exactly got heads.

She would get a book out of the library and find out.

When we get back to the world, she thought, not knowing how or when that would happen.

Her eyes moved back to the sleeping Josh. Again she wanted to wake him, tell him about the two children and the King's threat. She had discovered that he was not the king at all, but the Enemy. The real king was the one whose music made the world happen.

And Old Mother Alton . . . Josh himself had called her that.

A mother was what they both needed. That, and home. She could see the kitchen at home, with its row of decorated mugs that had once held Easter eggs. She could see the living room, and knew every piece of furniture, every knickknack. Once she had hardly noticed them. But she had dusted and polished them for weeks, months, and knew them all in detail: the little yellow jug with its chipped rim, the tapestry cushions of cats and birds, the bureau that had belonged to her grandmother.

Still there, she told herself, even if I can't see it. Any case—Mrs. Badger, now. And *this* is home.

TWELVE

Katy saw Ollie before he saw her. He was wandering, hands in pockets, down by the lake with its huge fake swans. She had been working her way clockwise around the park, looking for signs of the break-in. From a distance, right by the house itself, she had thought she saw a group of uniformed men—police, perhaps. But by the time she got there, they had gone.

She could not decide whether to go to Ollie or duck out of sight. He was unpredictable. She could hardly tell whose side he was on. He obeyed the King's orders, but unwillingly, it seemed.

He looked up and saw her, his pale face twisted and miserable. He looked enormously old and tired. She went to him.

"You see the King?"

She nodded.

"He tell you about the break-in?"

"Why did you *do* it?"

"What d'you think?" His voice was bitter. "He got me same as he's got you."

"What did you steal? Was it money?"

He looked at her and smiled faintly, then dug in his pocket. "Here. Take 'em." He held them out—the flashlight and a knife, the one Josh had used to carve the calendar on the tree. "Go on, take 'em—before I change my mind."

She obeyed.

"So you didn't—"

"I didn't do it."

"Oh, Ollie!" She could have hugged him. "Thanks! Oh, thank you!"

He shrugged. "Must be mad. Kill me when he finds out."

"Oh, Ollie!" Then, suddenly, "Would you like an ice cream?"

He stared, then laughed. "What—reward, you mean?"

"Yes—no. Would you? I mean, you can't pinch ice creams. Go on!"

Katy changed her ten-pound note to buy the ice creams. She saw his face when she pulled it out, and laughed. "Thought you'd got all our money, didn't you?"

"Crafty little beggar!"

They sat on the warm, damp grass, licking their ice creams, almost companionable.

"How old are you?" Katy asked.

"Sixteen. Listen, don't tell him!"

"Who? What?"

"The King. Don't let on I didn't do the job."

"Course not," she promised.

"Where's the little 'un? Off nicking?"

"Asleep. Not very well."

"All the more reason to clear off out of here. Why don't you?"

Katy did not reply, because to do so would mean telling of that other world in Alton. It would mean telling him that the King was not the king at all, but the Enemy.

"Look, I've been in homes—dozens of 'em—and all right, it's lousy. But it's better than this."

"But *you* ran away."

"Too right I did!"

"There you are, then! And you don't really want us to go, anyway. Leave you on your own with *him*. You said so."

He was looking at something beyond her.

"Rum-looking old biddy!"

She turned. It was the bag lady, trudging patiently and eternally, it seemed, going her secret errands.

"Oh, seen her before. Hey!" The thought struck her. "*You* can see her!"

"Not blind."

"No, but—" she stopped, still not sure how far she could trust him. "Have you seen her before?"

"Nope!"

Ollie had been here weeks, months even, and had never seen the bag lady before. She and Josh had seen her time and again. That man in the red coat had not seen her at all, or the security guards. Only the dog.

Animals, she knew, were supposed to have a sixth sense.

"I'm all of a puzzlement," she said.

He laughed. "Daft kid! Where'd you get that from?"

"My mum used to say it. 'I'm all of a puzzlement.'"

"Bet your mum's worried about you—being missing 'n' all."

"Probably doesn't know." She had expected the people at Kirby House to be worried—had meant them to be. Her mother had been so far removed for so long that Katy thought of her as inhabiting another world, almost. She looked directly at him.

"Are you our friend?"

He stared, then laughed awkwardly.

"*Are* you?" she persisted.

"What kind of daft question's that?"

"I know you're much older than us—so we can't be real friends, I s'pose. So . . . you could pretend we're your brother and sister!"

"*What?*"

"Family. Said you've got a little sister—same name, even."

"Nothing like her. Dead pretty she was, with yellow hair."

"You saying I'm ugly?"

He reached forward and tugged her hair, gently. "Werewolf! Elephant Man! Okay—I'm your friend. Must be, I s'pose. Told you—kill me if he finds out."

"*We* shan't tell him," Katy said.

"You want to watch out. More than just an ugly face, he is."

"What d'you mean?"

"Don't know. Not exactly. But . . . he ain't here just for the rides. He's up to something."

Katy said nothing.

"Only thing is—what?"

He jumped to his feet. "Better move on. Got eyes in the back of his head. Thanks for the ice, kid!"

Katy was left at a loose end. She went back to the den to see if Josh was awake. He lay exactly as she had left him, eyes closed, breathing gently.

Forgotten all about his calendar, she thought. Bet he never even did it yesterday.

She went out and found the tree with its single notch. Josh's knife was still in her pocket, so she took it out and carefully scored another, and another. She found it satisfying—a real thing to do, instead of just passing time.

"Yesterday—and today."

So it was Saturday—a whole week now since that first visit. A day when the park would be filled to overflowing. Better get down there quick if I want some rides. Lines a mile long!

She went out of the gardens and wandered between favorite rides. But it was all pointless.

Shouldn't think anyone ever comes here on their own, she thought. Everyone else was with families, friends—someone to laugh with and get terrified with. Probably what makes me stick out more than anything—being on my own.

She remembered the book she had promised herself and went to choose it, taking her time, hoping to find the kind of story you could finish, then start reading all over again. The kind of book you would take to a desert island.

Down by the lake she saw an empty seat. The sun was strong now, so she took off her jacket and laid it beside her, as if saving a place for someone. As she did so she checked the pockets, feeling the reassuring shape of the wooden doll. Then she opened the book and began to read, and after only a few pages the magic was working. She was out of Alton, out of the world. She had meant to ration herself, read only a couple of chapters and save the rest, but forgot about that, too, along with everything else.

"Hey!" There was a light tap on her head. She jumped, startled.

"What's all this? *Reading*—at Alton?"

It was a man with a red coat—the same one she had spoken to yesterday to ask about the bag lady.

"I've seen it all!" Then, "Haven't I seen you before?"

"No! No!" She jumped up. "Got to go—Mum'll be looking for me!"

"Hey—come back!" She heard him call after her, but ignored him. "Your coat!"

"Coat!" she gasped, and turned. He was holding out her jacket. She felt sick with all the sickness in the world. She had almost lost the wooden doll. She walked back, her legs suddenly weak.

"Thanks! Mum'd've killed me."

He looked at her hard.

She had not looked in a mirror for days, so could not tell what he was seeing. He saw a pale, streaked face and unwashed hair, grubby T-shirt and jeans, mud-caked sneakers. She did not look like a child got ready by a mother to go on an outing. Nor did she look like the photograph of herself that had been shown on television and in newspapers.

He shrugged. "Kids!" he said, and walked off.

She made instinctively for the gardens. Past the Log Flume she went, and was level with the Haunted House when she saw him. She stopped dead.

The King—the Enemy—unmistakable with his high cock's comb, was coming toward her. He had broken cover and was mingling with the Saturday crowds. She did not even stop to think. She darted into the Haunted House. She had not dared do so before, but there was no choice.

At once she was swept into a world of terror.

The air about her was thick with phantoms. It was no use telling herself that they were not real, because they were here, now, awful and compelling. She screamed, and her terror was the terror that had begun when she had seen the King advancing toward her. She was drawn deeper into nightmare, and there was no way out, and she screamed again.

She burst back into the daylight, gasping with relief. She sometimes read books to scare herself, but that was different. Then, you were in charge. You could stop when things got too much, and come back later. You could even not finish the book at all. In the Haunted

House there was no escape. You were in there, part of it, and you had to keep going in order to get out.

Bit like how we are now, me and Josh, she thought. Can't go back, can't stay where we are—got to go on.

The trouble was, she did not know how. In the real world there were rules. If you did certain things, then certain other things followed. If you poured boiling water on a tea bag, you got a cup of tea. If you did your best writing, the teacher was pleased with you. If you walked over a zebra crossing, the traffic stopped for you. Here, there were no rules—or at least, none that she could make sense of. She did not know what to do, how to make things turn out right.

She carried on back to the den, keeping an extracareful lookout. She stopped by the orangery to fill her water bottle. Josh might not be hungry, but he seemed to get thirsty. She remembered her own illnesses, in the past, when a jug of lemon-barley water would stand by her bed. She would drift in and out of sleep, hearing the buzz of a fly, the cars going by in the street, and the distant rattle of dishes down below. Now and then she would lift her head and gratefully sip the sweet-sour liquid. She remembered how enormously soft and friendly her bed had felt at those times—twice as big, twice as soft as at any other time.

Josh was still sleeping on the crumpled clothes he had spread over the garbage bag. At any rate, his eyes were closed.

"Josh!" she said softly. "Josh!"

He half opened his eyes.

"How d'you feel?"

"Head hurts. Throat."

"Here—drink this."

She unscrewed the bottle and held it out. He raised himself on an elbow. Katy watched as he tilted back his head and drank.

"Thanks." He handed her the bottle and sank back again.

Katy looked down at him, uncertain what to say or do. This limp, silent Josh was not the one she knew. He seemed almost a stranger.

"Saw Ollie," she told him.

"Who?"

"You know—Ollie. And guess what: He didn't do the break-in! Oh, of course—you don't even know!"

She realized that she had traveled a long way without him that morning. He knew nothing of her meeting with the two children at the stones; about Quantum, whose music made the world happen. He did not know about the King's threat, about the stolen flashlight and knife.

"Oh—I wish there was a grown-up!"

The words burst out without her even seeming to think them. It was only as she heard herself say them that she realized that they were true. Grown-ups made the rules, told you what to do. Even if you didn't like them, at least they made a sort of framework. They made the world safe.

"What'd you say?" he murmured. "What grown-up?"

"Nothing. Doesn't matter."

"Not going back . . . not ever . . ."

"We—Josh, we might have to!"

"No! No!" He half raised himself again, then dropped back. "Oh, my head. . . . No, Katy, no! *Please.*"

"All right," she said.

"Promise?"

She did not reply. A promise was a big thing.

"Promise," he insisted. His voice was a mere croak.

"Promise," she said helplessly.

He closed his eyes again.

"Oh, Josh, *do* get better!"

He seemed not to hear her. She found herself mad at him for leaving her alone. He was lucky, having a sort of holiday from the world. He was in a place where the King—the Enemy—could not touch him.

"You'll be better by teatime," she said, more for her own benefit than his.

It struck her that here even teatime did not exist. Breakfast, lunch, tea, bedtime, none of them did. They were adrift in a sea of time with no landmarks.

Her watch showed nearly half past one. At school they would all be lining up at the playground, to go back in. She wished she were there with them. Just for the afternoon, anyway, she excused herself. Then, Oh, no! It's Saturday!

She was as disappointed as if she really had been going on an outing, canceled at the last minute. She had wanted, just for a few hours, to be ordinary Katy, rather than Katy on the run. To be among people who knew her, rather than crowds of strangers, to sniff the familiar classroom smell of chalk and dust, instead of the powerful, foreign smells of earth and greenery.

"I've got some jobs to do!" she told the unconscious Josh. "I'm busy."

It was too hot to wear her jacket, and she knew now how easy it would be to lose it. She found a plastic bag in the jumble of belongings. Some were damp to the touch. She spread them out, hung the T-shirts on branches. She sniffed at them. Pooh! Make 'em smell better, anyhow!

The doll went into the bag, and she dropped a spare T-shirt over it and added the two water bottles, after emptying out the water left.

"Going to look for a newspaper," she announced. "See if we're in it." Josh made no sign. "And *get better!*" she told him, and went.

The security men were finishing their lunch break.

"Seen this?" Bill asked. "About that kid's mother?"

"What kid?"

"The two that's gone missing. One of 'em's mother was in the hospital."

"Oh. Yeah. Saw it on the TV."

"Says here she's out. 'Doctors amazed by mother's sudden recovery.'"

Dave grinned.

"'S in mine, too. Look!"

There was the headline: MIRACLE MUM BEATS BLUES.

"That's all very well," Bill said, "but what if they

don't find 'em? Back in the blues then, and no mistake."

"Like looking for a needle in a haystack. Anywhere, they could be. . . ."

THIRTEEN

Katy wandered about the park that afternoon looking for a newspaper. She saw plenty, frustratingly thrust into bags and pockets or being read, but searched the bins in vain. She found some chips and a couple of egg sandwiches, and ate them.

The air in the valley was still and warm. Before long she felt her eyelids heavy. Could be getting the same thing as Josh!

She swallowed once or twice very carefully, testing her throat for soreness. Feels all right.

But she could not fight off the drowsiness. On the sloping green by the lake, she lay down and shut her eyes. In the end she slept.

She did not see the shadows that fell across her twice during that afternoon. First, that of a cloaked figure came, paused, and passed on. The second was longer, thinner, the shadow of a man. That stayed longer before it, too, passed on.

When she awoke, Katy could not for a moment think where she was. Her cheek was pressed on grass;

it was still light. She sat up, blinking. Down the paths, over the lawns, people were streaming in the same direction.

Nearly closing time!

She must hurry back to the gardens, cut across the tide of visitors. Home for her did not lie in the same direction. She went first to the orangery and refilled the two bottles.

In the den she found Josh exactly as she had left him. She looked down at him, unable to believe that anyone could sleep for so long, let alone Josh. As she watched, he flung out an arm and muttered, and she thought he said, "Higher, higher!" She dropped to her knees, stretched out a hand, and felt his forehead, as so often her mother had felt hers.

Hot! She knew it was a bad sign. It was a sign that would send her mother hurrying for the thermometer—for the doctor, even. There were other memories.

Water! She delved into her bag for her toilet things, and found the washcloth. Then, unscrewing the water bottle, she wet it. She looked dubiously down at Josh then, and very gently drew the wet cloth across his forehead. He made no sign. Emboldened, she wiped his whole face, his neck. It was like washing a doll.

She took one of his hands, meaning to wipe that, too. For an instant it felt soft, floppy, and then her own hand was being gripped by it, hot and tight. Then his eyes opened wide, and he was muttering, talking in snatches.

"Josh! Are you all right?"

She saw with horror that although his eyes were open, they were not seeing.

"I gotta go. I gotta go," he muttered, and his head twisted this way and that.

"Go where, Josh?" She tried to withdraw her hand, but still he held it, tightly, fiercely.

"Lots, oh, lots of 'em!"

"Lots of what?"

"Don't go! Coming . . . coming . . ." And he shot up suddenly, startling her. He let go of her hand. He was staring into the wall of leaves and seeing things invisible to her. "Ah, there . . . no . . . get off, get off!" He seemed terrified, eyes glaring.

She raked swiftly through her things and found a plastic cup and half filled it.

"There they go! Go on—get off!" He sank back again, his breath coming in little pants.

She held out the cup, but he did not take it.

"I'll help you." With one arm she raised his head, burning and heavy. She put the cup to his lips, and he drank as if in a dream. He lapped and lapped, then gave a gasp, and she lowered his head gently again. "That's better," she said. "You'll be better now."

"Daft little beggars! Look at 'em; look at 'em! Lots of little skipping angels—look at 'em! Up and down like yo-yos! Daft little beggars. . . ." His voice sank to a murmur. His eyes were closed again.

"Oh, Josh, don't go!" she begged.

But he was deaf. She stared down at him.

"I'll try and make you comfy," she said, and began tidying his makeshift bed.

The last monorail had gone, taking the last visitors to the car park. Besides Katy and Josh, only three visitors remained. One stood in a high room of the Towers, looking out through a stone window over his kingdom, smiling faintly. From time to time he looked at his watch, and frowned.

The person he was expecting was hiding in the park, keeping on the move. From cover to cover he went, white-faced, yellow-haired, and long-legged as a crane. He did not see that other figure that also wove a pattern through the gardens—slow, steady, bent on a secret errand.

The valley was warm and still and eerily hushed. The birds were invisible and silent.

The evening wore on. In the den, Katy heard the first distant rumble of thunder.

"Oh, no!" she whispered, and raised her eyes fearfully. Josh tossed and whimpered. From time to time she wiped his forehead with the washcloth. It was growing darker by the minute—an early, unnatural darkness. Then came the first wide yawn of lightning, followed by a crack of thunder.

"We're under trees! You're not supposed to be under trees in a storm!"

She looked upward, and again there was a flash of lightning, and she saw the leaves and twigs go into a shiver, fringed with brilliance before the darkness came again, and the thunder.

Josh muttered, "Where . . . don't know where . . ."

"It's all right. I'm here. There's no need to be frightened. You're more likely to be run over by a car than struck by lightning, Miss Carpenter says. She says it's millions to one. It's—"

She yelped as lightning tore the sky again and was followed by a deafening clap of thunder.

"How many miles away? Count—count the seconds, that's it! Always further away than you think, Miss Carpenter says. Count after the next flash. . . ."

The den was lit momentarily, and she saw Josh's eyes, wide-open and glittering.

"One . . . two . . . three . . . four . . . five . . . six . . .," she counted rapidly. Thunder. "Six miles! Safe as houses." But she knew that she had cheated. "No—counted too quick—oh! One . . . two . . . three . . ." A crack of thunder. Then the rain came, spattering heavily. "Oh, no! No!"

She groped about for the garbage bag she had sat on earlier. It was wet and slippery. She tried to spread it over Josh, but he flung it off, moaning.

"Oh, lie still, please, please! Oh, you'll get soaked!"

Next time the lightning and the thunder were almost simultaneous; the "One . . ." was hardly out of her mouth. It was too much. She scrambled to her feet and pushed through the dripping foliage.

"Help!" she screamed. "Help—oh, somebody, help!"

Desperately she scanned about, the rain half blinding

her. She could not leave Josh lying there alone. Who would hear her, here in the teeming gardens? The lightning tore the sky again and lit the valley a chill moon white.

"Help!" she sobbed. "Oh, please, please, somebody!"

Help came. In the next flare she saw two figures hurrying, one behind the other.

"Oh, thank goodness; thank goodness! Here! Here!"

The bag lady's cloak swirled around her. Ollie's hair was lank and dripping.

"Quick—in here!"

She led the way into the den. Ollie lifted Josh, limp and silent, easily into his arms.

"The doll!" Katy snatched it up and thrust it into the pocket of her jacket.

The bag lady was waiting on the path. She made a beckoning sign and went on, cloak streaming behind her, from time to time haloed in bluish light. They drew level with the orangery, and Ollie paused.

"Thought we were . . . going there!" he gasped, jerking his head toward it.

"No! No! Follow her!"

The strange foursome trudged onward, heads bent against the rain. On they went until at last they reached the stones. Katy lifted her eyes to see them against a streaked silver-and-navy sky. The bag lady's cloak lifted and flapped—and she disappeared. One minute she was there, a dark, ragged shape—the next gone.

Then Katy, too, crossed the invisible line, and the world and the weather were snuffed out like a candle.

She stood in the calm and sunlight and let out a long, shuddering breath.

"What—what the—?" Ollie, still cradling Josh in his arms, looked about him in disbelief. From somewhere in the distance came the laughter and shouts of children.

"So now you know," said Katy.

She herself had known that the only possible place to fly to was the stones. But she had not known whether they would find Quantum and the flying lights, or the children.

"At night, you can always come. You knew that?" Matt had said. But although the valley had been darkened by the storm, it was not night properly; not yet.

Ollie still stood staring and shaking his head. "But . . . I do not believe it! What the—? Where's *she*?"

"I don't know," Katy told him, "but she's done it before."

"Done what?"

"Vanished. Here."

"Must be going off my nut. Ain't dreaming, am I?"

"What about him?" she indicated Josh. "He's no dream."

He looked down. Josh's eyes were closed.

"Is he . . . is he all right?"

"He will be. Now that he's here."

Gently Ollie lowered Josh to the ground. He straightened and looked about him. "I don't get it. These stones—they're Alton."

"I think there's more than one Alton," Katy said.

"So where's the rest of it? Where's that storm?"

"Just wait—wait till you see the king."

He was on guard, eyes flicking nervously about. "The *what*?"

"The *real* king," she told him. "Quantum. The one whose music makes the world happen."

"I give up." He sat then, on the grass by Josh. "One thing: It feels safe here."

"It is." She drew the carved doll from her pocket.

"What's that?"

She smiled. "Passport. Sort of."

"Get real! Passport!"

"You wait here, with Josh," she said. "I'm going to look for someone."

Somewhere, not far away, would be Beth and Matt. She went from among the stones and saw the same valley that she and Josh had seen by moonlight. It lay green and sunlit, and the only sounds were bird song and the echoing laughter and cries of children. Now they were singing.

> "The good ship sails through the Illey Alley O,
> The Illey Alley O,
> The Illey Alley O,
> The good ship sails through the Illey Alley O
> On the last day of September."

"There you are!"

Katy turned, and there they were, both of them.

"Did she bring you here? Old Mother Alton?"

"And then vanished! Why does she always vanish?"

"She guards the other world—your world," Matt told her. "Hadn't you guessed?"

"She do come and go," Beth said. "But Quantum, he's always here."

"But he isn't!" said Katy. "I've just come from the stones, and he isn't!"

"You mean you didn't see him," Matt told her. "That's nothing. Any more than he sees you."

"He's blind," Beth said.

"Blind?" Katy had a swift picture of that first time she had seen him, and could have sworn his eyes met hers.

"Can't tell day from night—"

"Summer from winter—"

"Century from century—"

There was a little silence. Far away the children were singing a new song.

> "Two, two, the lily-white boys,
> Clothed all in green, ho-ho.
> One is one and all alone
> And evermore shall be, so!"

"The Enemy . . ." Matt said.

"He's after the harp!" Beth said. "You must stop him; you must!"

"If once he gets that, we're all in his power," Matt said.

"I think he knows," Katy said. "That he needs us—Josh and me."

"He can't get here unless you bring him," he told her.

"Or unless—unless—" Beth pointed to her doll. "You must keep it safe!"

"We'll never bring him," Katy said, "Unless . . . he makes us. . . ."

They stared at one another, all three.

"Or unless . . . he could find someone else. Been looking for a kid for ages, Ollie says. Ollie's our friend—he's much older, but he's on our side now. He must be—the bag lady—I mean Old Mother Alton—she fetched him to us."

"There *is* a way," said Matt slowly. "A way to get rid of the Enemy forever."

"Oh, no! Don't, don't!" Beth clapped her hands over her ears and shut her eyes.

"The black hole."

"You mean—you mean there's a *real* one?"

"Ask her." He jerked his head toward the cowering Beth.

"Brother disappeared into it."

"But—but that was *ages* ago—must've been!"

"Black holes don't just happen," he said. "They're *there* and always have been. Ask any of the kids here."

Katy's head spun. She remembered what Josh had said: "Hey. . . . People *vanish* in there! . . . Pff! Gone! Whizzing around in outer space!"

"But listen," she said, "there *is* a ride—the Black Hole."

"I know," said Matt calmly. "Been on it."

"Millions of people go on it, and they don't disappear."

"They would," he told her, "if it wasn't for the music. Don't you see—it's Quantum versus the Enemy. Why d'you think the Enemy's after the harp?"

Katy stared at him, horrified. "You mean if he gets it, stops the music—"

"The Black Hole swallows 'em! And that's what he wants—the Enemy!"

"Then he'll be king again! Oh, I can't bear it, I can't!" Beth started to cry.

"Don't cry," said Katy. "We won't let it happen. We won't."

Then the music began.

"Listen!" she said, and as she spoke the world slowly darkened. "I remember when we first heard that."

"And me," said Matt. "It's how he calls the children."

"What children?" Katy asked.

"Any that need him. Haven't you noticed—the valley's full of children."

"All fetched here by Old Mother Alton. She's his eyes, see."

"I want to see him again," Katy said. "Quantum."

They turned toward the stones, and in the near darkness could see the lights being pulled out of nowhere by the fingered harp. As they drew near, Katy saw Ollie, crouched by Josh's sleeping form and staring into the light.

They went forward and sat wordless, watching and listening. Quantum's shock of snowy hair sprang from his head like wires; his eyes gazed sightless; all his power ran from the tips of his fingers and into the strings.

"He's got us all in the palm of his hand," Matt whispered, and Katy believed it. The whole valley, the wakeful owls and slinking fox, the children out there in the dark woods, even the drifting clouds, all were poised at the music's edge. The least faltering, the touch of a wrong note, could send them all tumbling into chaos.

That was the moment when Katy knew that they must stay, and fight the Enemy.

FOURTEEN

Katy awoke in another different place. She gazed up and saw the stones rearing into a pearl sky. She sat up and saw that Josh and Ollie were lying nearby, still sleeping.

We fell asleep listening to the music. They had fallen asleep in another time, or at least in the dream of another time. "It's a mystery!"

"Katy?" It was Josh.

"Josh! You all right?"

"Think so. Cor, feel as if I've been asleep for years." He smiled ruefully, lifted his head, then dropped back again. "Feel like a sack of old potatoes!"

She laughed. She could have hugged him because he was himself again, instead of a shivering, blank-eyed stranger.

"Frightened the life out of me!" she said. "Thought you were going to *die*!" Now she dared admit it.

He was gazing upward, puzzled. "The stones! What're we doing here?"

"Wish I knew. Well, I do really. But . . . he brought you." She indicated the huddled form of Ollie.

"Ollie! *He* did? What—"

"There was a storm, a terrific one. Don't you remember?"

"'Member something. . . ." He frowned. "We been *there* again? That old geezer with the harp?"

"Quantum. Yes. Oh, there's millions of things to tell you. But we must get back. Anyone could find us here."

"Hungry," he murmured. "Ravenous."

She laughed again. This was definitely the old Josh talking.

"Hey! You two!" It was Ollie, tousled and blinking.

"Help!" He was on his feet. "Come on—out here, quick!"

Katy scrambled to her feet. "Can you get up, Josh?"

"Try . . ." He raised himself on one arm. "Giddy . . . wow . . . worse'n the Corkscrew."

"Come on, tiger." Ollie crouched by Josh. "Arms around my neck."

Then Josh was hoisted on Ollie's back and the three of them were hurrying away, down into the silent gardens toward the safety of the den.

Left lying there, blankly gazing up at the sky, was the gingerbread shape of the wooden doll.

Ollie deposited Josh on the tumbled heap of clothes and plastic bags.

"There you go! Home sweet home!"

He straightened up and looked at Katy. "Was I dreaming, or what? That old guy with the music—all them lights?"

"Not dreaming," she told him.

"Hungry . . ." murmured Josh again.

"Same here," said Ollie. "You 'n' me had better go. Back soon, tiger!"

The pair hurried through the gardens, gorgeous now in the first sun: a wet green blaze. The air was icy and pierced with cuckoo calls; the whole valley was filled with a huge excitement.

"Now you know," said Katy, hurrying to keep up.

"Know *nothing*! What's it all about?"

"Quantum—the harp. It's what the Enemy's after."

"Enemy?"

"It's who he is. He might call himself the King, but he's not. He's the Enemy."

"He's that, all right," said Ollie grimly. "Out for blood, and no mistake."

"There's something you don't know," she told him. "About the other Alton."

"You can say that again."

"It's full of children. Like Josh and me."

"Mmm. Thought I heard 'em. Like them two last night?"

"Yes. But there's something else. You—you're not going to believe it."

"What?" He stopped and looked at her, waiting.

"A black hole!"

When they had raided the bins by the kiosks, Ollie said, "Let's go and take a look."

"What at?"

"This black hole."

Katy hesitated. To get there they would have to go deeper into the park, past the Towers itself. There was the risk of being seen, not only by staff, but by the Enemy. On the other hand, she was irresistibly curious. She wondered whether now that she knew there was a real black hole, she would be able, somehow, to tell.

"All right. But better be quick. Trucks'll be here soon, and Josh is hungry, remember."

The Black Hole, with its green-and-white striped dome, looked exactly as it always had. Katy pictured it with its waiting line at one side, and at the other a succession of people reeling out, white and shaken or jubilant and yelling.

"I can't believe it," she said.

"Believe what?" inquired a soft voice.

She turned. There, towering over her, was the Enemy. She dropped back, clutching the bag of food.

"N-nothing!" she stammered.

"Oh, I think so," he said.

"Morning, chief!" said Ollie. He patted his own bag. "Got the rations."

"Had a good night, did we?" said the Enemy. "Get any further?"

"I should say so."

"Getting warm, are we?"

"Oh, very warm, chief. Nearly there, I'd say."

Katy, horror-struck, looked from one to the other. Ollie did not even look at her.

"You'd better tell me about it," said the Enemy.

Katy fled. As she ran, she expected a rough hand on her shoulder at any moment, but none came.

He tricked us, he tricked us! she thought as she ran.

Ollie, who had rescued them in the storm and seemed their friend, had betrayed them. He was not on their side at all. He was what he had always been—the right-hand man of the Enemy.

"So now what?" she said bitterly.

Josh, who had managed two potatoes, lay listening to her story.

"I liked Ollie," he said.

"He *meant* us to. He tricked us. All that stuff about the break-in—it was just a trick."

"He carried me on his back. Called me tiger."

"Oh, Josh—what shall we do?"

"We'll think of something, Katy."

"Oh, *yes*!"

"But not yet. Still feel wobbly."

She looked at him. "They'll be plotting against us, at this very minute—him and Ollie!"

"But they can't get there without us."

"That's true," she said slowly. "Or without—oh, he even knows about this!"

She put her hand into the pocket of her jacket. A great coldness swept over her.

"The doll!" she whispered. "It's gone!"

She actually shivered. When and where had she last seen it? She remembered snatching it up as they had left the den in the storm. She remembered taking it out at the stones, and showing it to—Ollie.

"I showed it to him! I told him it was a passport!"

"I liked Ollie," said Josh again sadly, to himself, almost.

"And then—and then—I still had it when I met the others, and Beth—"

"What?"

"She said to keep it safe. Oh, Josh!" Tears sprang to her eyes.

"Don't cry, Katy. Might still be there."

"Where?"

"By the stones. Where we slept. Anywhere."

"But even if Ollie hasn't got it—*we* haven't, either! We can't get back there."

"Can at night—"

"That might be too late! And the Enemy—he'd be watching us! He knows!"

"But if he's got the doll, he don't need us," Josh murmured, sleepy again. "Passport, remember."

She jumped to her feet. "I'm going to look for it. It's our only chance."

She pushed through the wet boughs, and they closed behind her. It was still not nine o'clock, but she hardly remembered that she was meant to be in hiding. Things had changed. She no longer thought of herself and Josh as just runaways. Now they were something else as well. Now they were the only ones who could save the valley from the Enemy. They were guardians of the music that made the world happen.

The stones stood calm and rooted; the air among them was innocent and fresh. Not a trace remained of the night's happenings. Katy ran this way and that like a tracking dog, eyes fixed to the ground. The doll was not there.

"Oh, *oh!*" She stamped her foot, stamped as if she wished she could make the earth rock. "You're still there, somewhere!" she cried to the empty air. "I know you are. Listen—I'm sorry; I'm sorry!"

No sign, no answer.

Tears were streaming now. "I'm sorry," she whispered, and walked away into the garden, into the Alton that was here and now, the Alton that contained not only herself and Josh, but the Enemy.

She had so hoped against hope that the doll would be there, among the stones, that she only now remembered that still she might find it. It could be lying anywhere on the paths she had taken that morning: between here and the den, between the den and the kiosks, then the Black Hole itself. She lowered her eyes and kept them down till she reached the den.

Josh had his eyes closed again.

"Josh!"

He opened them, but only a little.

"It's not there—at the stones. But I've thought: I ran all the way back from the Black Hole. Could've jumped out of my pocket."

"Could've," he agreed drowsily.

"So I'll have to go back there. Now."

There was no response.

"Oh, I wish you weren't poorly!"

He grinned faintly. "Can't ezackly help it. . . ."

"But—keep your fingers crossed for me!"

She walked out through the wall of leaves and began

to retrace her earlier steps toward the kiosks. Never before had she so desperately wanted to find a lost thing. She summoned all the magic she could muster.

"Only on shadows, only on shadows!" she muttered. "If I only step on shadows, I'll find it!"

She stepped from shadow to shadow, scanning the path until her eyes ached. She began to make promises to herself, as she often had when she was little. She no longer really believed in this, but it was at least a comfort.

Let me find it, and I'll stop biting my nails! This was a promise she had made many times and never managed to keep. But I will this time, I promise!

She was halfway through the gardens now. She cast around for another sacrifice. There was very little she could give up, here and now, because she had so little.

My book! If I find the doll, I'll take the book and chuck it in a bin! She doubted whether this sounded like much to whatever fates might be listening. And I've hardly got into it, and I'm dying to know what happens. I'll chuck it in a bin, *and* my flashlight. "Oh!" She stopped, startled, as a squirrel streaked across her path.

"Oh, *now* look what you've made me do!"

She had stepped clear into a patch of sunlight. The charm was broken. Her eyes followed the squirrel into the bushes, with a shiver of leaves. Then it reappeared, running easily up a tree trunk.

Wish I was a squirrel! How marvelous, how gay and freewheeling to be that silvery, flashing thing!

Right up the tree it scampered, as if it were climbing to the sky. Katy shaded her eyes against the sun to track it. She saw not the squirrel, but that raggedy black shape falling slowly out of the sky. Down it came, foreign and familiar, a mystery.

Then, all at once, she knew. The bag lady.

The old woman crossed and recrossed between that other Alton and this. She went there simply by stepping in among the stones, and returned as easily, flying like a bird. Back and forth she shuttled, going where she was needed, doing her work. And all in silence, all without a single word ever being spoken.

Come to help me and Josh! It was as if an enormous weight had been lifted. She and Josh had a part to play in saving the invisible children of the valley, and those other children who came here day by day, never knowing the danger they were in. But they were not alone.

Katy did not go in search of the bag lady. She knew that she planned her own entrances and exits. In any case, there was still the doll to find. That, surely, was part of her own task. She had lost it and she must find it.

On she went, eyes fixed again on the path with its wet littered leaves and little shining puddles.

Let me find it, let me find it, let me find it! The refrain ran in her head. But she did not make any more promises.

FIFTEEN

So lost was Katy in her task, so intent on finding the doll, that she did not notice the men till it was almost too late. She heard them before she saw them. By then she had almost reached the kiosks. Hearing voices, she looked up, startled, and there they were, advancing toward her.

Oh! She stepped swiftly off the path, and in the same moment one of the men raised his head. Katy tried to push further into the shrubbery, but it was too dense, and so she crouched low, willing herself invisible.

"Funny!" she heard.

"What?"

"Could've sworn . . ."

"What?"

"Could've sworn I saw a kid!"

A laugh.

The smell of wet earth, nettles, leaves was overpowering. She was like a fox in its den. She prayed that the dog was not with them. There was no bag lady to save her this time.

"Seeing things, Bill. You and the dog both."

"Could've sworn. A girl, it was."

There was a swishing as boughs were parted. A spatter from wet leaves.

"Oh, yes? Got wings, had she?"

Another swish of branches.

"Come *on*!"

Katy held her breath. There were receding footsteps.

"Breakfast."

"Better hand this in to Lost Props, I s'pose."

"Hardly worth it, I should've thought."

The voices faded. Katy straightened, and a little shower came down.

Lost Props! The—doll?

It was perfectly possible, she realized. Those men, and others, patrolled the park day and night. They had been coming from the direction of the kiosks. The doll could have slipped out of her pocket as she crouched over the bags, earlier, lifting food. They could've found it—not the Enemy!

By now it was nearly nine. Already the park was coming alive. Soon the first visitors would be rushing through the turnstiles. The Enemy would have gone to ground.

She waited before going into the park proper. She waited until there were enough other children to act as cover, to make her as good as invisible. Even then it was too early, she knew, to go to Lost Property. She found herself wandering, without really planning it, toward the Black Hole.

There she stood at a distance and watched. Gangs of friends, whole families, were going in there, some laughing, some clutching at one another in terror, half mock, half real. They could not know that they were on the very fringes of the world, that before them yawned a pit. A black void was waiting to swallow them.

They think it's just another ride.

If the worst happened, if the Enemy won and the music stopped, she wondered how many children would tumble out of the world and into nowhere? And who then could plug that hole, make Alton safe again? Her heart began to thud. She wanted to rush forward and warn them: Look out, look out! Don't go in there!

She marked one family: mother, father, girl in a bright yellow tracksuit. They went in.

Katy ran around to the other side and waited. Time ticked by; she heard it inside her head—seconds, minutes. Then they were there, the mother holding her head, father laughing, girl staggering from side to side.

Much they know! Katy thought, and wondered what she would have done had they *not* come out? And if they had not, neither would anyone ever again.

Yet this was how it would happen. A perfectly ordinary day, a clear blue sky, and children lining up to disappear forever.

There was still time to pass somehow before she could go to Lost Property. She wandered off into Talbot Street, with its penny arcade and doll museum.

Dolls! She entered, not for a moment imagining that

she might find her doll, the one she was looking for. But there might be one like it!

That at least would prove something. It would prove that once, in the far-off past, there had been dolls so roughly carved from wood that they hardly resembled human beings at all. It would prove that the other Alton was not a shared dream, a nothing.

She was soon dizzied by the fixed eyes of dolls with painted faces. Blue, gray, brown, painted, or glass, they stared at her, followed her. There was something uncanny in their very number, as if the hundreds of them combined in one powerful, unwinking gaze.

She found herself wondering what it would be like in there at night, among those stiff and silent dummies. Once, children had played with them, giving them names and a kind of life of their own. Perhaps traces of that life lingered on, gathering in the darkness, quickening the echoes of old games. Perhaps those stares were no longer blank but alive, watchful. She would not want to walk among those dolls alone at night.

She escaped from the museum with relief, still feeling eyes boring into her back.

Lost Property.

This now seemed her only hope. She searched in vain for it on her map, but guessed that it would be somewhere near the entrance. That was where Lost Children was marked, and they, she supposed, were Lost Property of a sort. She made her way there, past the lake, Kiddies' Kingdom, and the farm.

She went along Towers Street, past the gift shops and the jumping fountain. Ahead, visitors were swarming in, and a jazz band played. Outside the Lost Children office she paused, summoning up her courage. By entering that door she would be reentering the real world. She had been so long away from it that she felt like a foreigner.

I must. The doll could be there. It's my last chance.

She went in. A woman was talking on the telephone, and she smiled at Katy and whispered, "Shan't be a minute, dear!" before carrying on her conversation. In a corner was a television set, switched on and showing the news. That, too, was a shock, another reminder of the real world.

"Now, dear, what can I do for you? Never lost—a big girl like you!"

"Oh, no, no. It's just—are you Lost Property, please?"

"I'm Lost everything—kids, property. . . . What is it you've lost? Bit early yet for anything to be handed in."

"It's . . . a doll."

"Doll? One you've bought, you mean? Didn't leave it in the shop, did you?"

"No! No, it's an old one. Very. Carved out of wood."

The woman eyed her dubiously. "Nothing like that's been handed in, dear. Unless . . . I suppose one of Security might've—hang on; I'll ask."

She disappeared through a door behind her. Katy turned her attention back to the television screen. Her heart stopped. There, impossibly, was her mother.

"Yes, I am," she was saying. "The doctors think it may have been the shock. *Real* shock treatment, they said." She smiled. She actually smiled, for a moment.

"It all seems like a bad dream now, looking back on it. And Katy—I keep thinking, what must it have been like for her?"

It's Mum! It's really Mum!

It was the mother she remembered best, the one she had kept telling herself would one day come back from behind the plate glass of misery.

"And if you could speak to Katy now, what would you say to her?"

Her mother looked straight into the camera. "Come home, Katy. Just that: Please, please come home!"

"Oh, Mum!" The screen went into a blur. She hardly noticed the door reopening, the woman returning.

"I'm sorry, dear. The only thing Security's found's this, and—oh!"

Katy had turned and blundered out, leaving the door wide open behind her. The woman looked down at the cheap watch she was holding, then at the television. It showed two photographs side by side, a boy and a girl.

". . . or if you have any suspicions, here is the number to call. . . ."

The woman frowned. She went over to the open door and peered left and right. The small girl with the tear-streaked face and unkempt hair and clothes was nowhere in sight.

"Surely not . . . ," she murmured. "Not *here* . . ."

She closed the door and walked back to the desk. She stared thoughtfully for a moment at the telephone before lifting it, and starting to dial.

★   ★   ★

Katy ran straight back to the den.

"Josh! I've seen Mum; I've seen Mum!"

He was reading her book. *"What?"*

"On the TV! And she's better—oh, Josh, she smiled!"

"What about my mum?" His face was eager, hopeful. Katy did not answer.

"Bet she was on as well!"

"I . . . ran out. P'r'aps she was on after."

He made a face. "What's she say, anyhow? Your mum?"

"She said, 'Come home, Katy!' Oh Josh, I can go home—now, this very minute!"

"What about me?"

"They can't send me back to Kirby now, or anywhere else! Oh—I could be home by lunchtime!"

"My mum ain't a fit person."

His words finally reached her. "Oh, Josh!"

"No use her saying come home. They wouldn't let me."

"You—you could come home with me! Mum'd let you; I know she would!"

"Oh, yeah? And Kev and Micky, I s'pose. Nah. Back to Kirby."

Katy hated Josh's mother for not being a fit person. Her own joy was already fading. She had remembered she could not go home, with or without Josh.

"Any case, can't go; not yet."

He looked up at her.

"The Enemy. Quantum. There's only you and me can do it."

"You find the doll?"

She shook her head.

"Bet he's got it. The Enemy."

"Ollie must've pinched it."

"We're done for, then."

"Not just us! Matt, Beth—all those children!"

"Wish *he'd* fall in a black hole!" Josh said savagely.

She stared. "That's it!"

"What?"

"Somehow—oh, my brain's not working. Somehow we must get the Enemy in there!"

"But there ain't a black hole," Josh said. "That's the whole point."

"There is! It's only the music that stops it working. But if the music stopped—"

"Oh, yeah—great idea! Get the Enemy in there—don't ask me how—then stop the music, then—whoosh!"

"Yes!"

"Off he whizzes into the Black Hole, and about fifty kids with him! *Great* idea!"

"Oh. Yes." She had not thought of that.

"That'd give the cops some kids to look for!"

"All right, then—do it at night, when there aren't any kids."

"It don't *work* at night, bonehead."

"I *know* it doesn't. But the music—it makes the world happen."

"Whatever that means."

"*I* don't know what it means, either. But if it's true—really true—Quantum could do it!"

Josh lay back again and closed his eyes. "Oh, *I* don't know. Head hurts. . . ."

Katy looked at him. He was going back to sleep. She wanted desperately to go home, but there was work to do first. She was seized by the urge to do something—anything—but could not think what. Somewhere out there were the Enemy and Ollie, and somewhere was that other Alton, the valley of children. It would be night before she could go there again, now that she had lost the passport, the doll.

All the same, it was toward the stones she made. On her way she remembered the calendar tree. Josh's knife was still in her pocket. Carving a notch to mark another day was something to do. Time in the valley ran like quicksilver, but a day was still a day, and something that could be measured.

She took out the knife. She did not know that she was being watched. She put the tip of the blade to the bark.

"Ticktock goes the clock!" a soft voice said.

She whirled about. He watched her mockingly, legs akimbo, arms folded.

Katy made to run, but he stepped to block her way.

"You know," he said. "Don't you?"

She gulped and nodded.

"You know how to get there."

Her mind was working fast. She did not have a real plan. Almost without knowing why, she said, "But . . . it's only for children."

"Ah—children!"

"You're a grown-up. You can't get there."

She dodged suddenly past him and ran, but he was after her. He caught hold of her shoulder.

"There *is* a way!" he hissed. "Must be! You find it!" He shook her, hard. "You hear me?"

Again, words were out without her really thinking them at all.

"I . . . think . . . there is another way."

"What? *What?*"

She drew a deep breath. "The Black Hole!"

He released her so suddenly that she almost fell.

"Who—told—you?" The words came fierce and gritted.

"Nobody! I just—I just heard them!"

"Heard who?"

"The—the children!"

"Ah! The children!" He smiled, or rather curled his lips. "*They* should know. Into everything, kids are— they'll get what's coming to them!"

Katy, cornered like a fox, was as cunning as one. She waited, saying nothing.

"So . . . Black Hole . . . what about it?"

Still she stayed silent. What she was going to tell him must seem to be forced out of her, against her will.

He gripped her arm, tightly, and squeezed. She gasped with the pain. "Don't, oh, don't!"

"What—about—it?"

"At—at midnight!"

He stared, disbelieving. "Liar! It's not working then. Nothing is." He shook her again.

"It does. It—it works if someone goes in!"

He was looking at her intently, as if to read her mind. She forced herself to meet those cruel eyes.

"It—*what*?"

"Works. At midnight. And it takes you there. The music stops."

"Music! You've seen it—the harp!"

She nodded.

"It's mine! Mine!" He shook her again. "Say it!"

"It's . . . yours!" The words were barely a whisper.

"At midnight? It starts working, and it takes you there?"

Again she nodded.

"How do I know you're not lying?" He gave her another long glare, then thrust her away. He smiled then, that terrible thin smile. "You had better not be. Kids! They'll get what's coming to them!"

In the silence came men's voices, quite close.

"Get lost!" He pushed her roughly, and himself loped away.

Katy ran in among the bushes and crouched there.

"Poor old Marge. Got lost kids on the brain."

"Wonder she didn't ring the fuzz straight off."

"Lost her marbles. If it was one of those kids, why'd she go asking after lost dolls? *Very* likely. Still, she's not the only one. You were seeing things, earlier."

"Think the boss'll report it?"

"Dunno. Not exactly good for the image, is it—place swarming with cops. . . ."

Katy peered through the leaves at their retreating backs. Coming toward them—slowly, steadily—was the bag lady. Katy held her breath.

SIXTEEN

The security men did not see the bag lady, or if they did, they gave no sign. Katy stepped out of the shrubbery and stood waiting. The bag lady halted.

"Oh, thank goodness!" Katy could have hugged her. "I don't know what to do! I've lost the doll!"

The bag lady surveyed her thoughtfully.

"I think *he* might've got it—the Enemy."

The bag lady's face was calm. She made no sign.

"Look, you might not talk, but you can listen! And *you* can go there, anytime you want. So listen, can you take a message?"

There was a long pause, while birds whistled and the Thunder Looper sighed.

Slowly, very slowly, that ancient head was nodding.

"I've made a trap—for the Enemy! I told him the only way to get . . . there . . . is the Black Hole. Midnight, I told him."

The head tilted like a bird's.

"Tell Quantum! Tell him to stop the music. At midnight."

Now the head was nodding again.

"Oh, I *wish* you'd speak to me! It will work, won't it? The harp—the music that makes the world happen! Is it true? Is it true?"

She had to ask the question, though she knew there would be no real answer. The bag lady nodded; she nodded and moved on.

Katy stood watching her, then, on impulse, ran after her. "I know who you really are—you're Old Mother Alton. So listen—I've seen *my* mother! And I'm going home soon. Oh, I'm going home!"

The old woman looked at her, and her gaze seemed sorrowful, reproachful.

"Oh—but not yet! Don't look at me like that! We'll save the music and the other children—tell them!"

Then the bag lady plodded on again, on her way to the stones and that other Alton.

Josh was asleep. He did not see the stirring of leaves that meant someone was entering the den.

The intruder stood gazing down at him. His high cock's comb gleamed in the sunlight shafting down through the high trees. His gaze moved over the tumbled piles of clothes and bags, then rested on Josh, thumb in mouth, sprawled on a rumpled garbage bag.

Then, without warning, he moved. He stooped and scooped Josh swiftly up, a hand clamped over his mouth. Josh's eyes opened and looked wildly up at him, and little urgent cries of protest were trapped in his mouth and throat.

The Enemy pushed through the springing branches and strode off, fast and silent. He stepped through the gardens, moving from cover to cover, eyes wary, knowing where he was going. The park was his kingdom, and he knew it well. He knew secret places where no visitors ever came, lairs where he lay low, like a fox or badger.

His hostage struggled feebly at first, then went limp. The Enemy looked down and saw the dangling head and closed eyes, and smiled.

"Josh!" Katy called. "Josh?"

Surely by now he had had enough sleep. She had been dying for the past hour to tell him of her meeting with the Enemy, and then the bag lady. She burst through the leaves and saw the den empty.

"Josh?"

Silly to say his name again. Of course he was not playing tricks, hiding.

There was a piece of paper by the garbage bag, and she picked it up, thinking it might be a message. It was blank. She turned it over. WATCH IT. It was the first sign they had had that they were being watched, days ago—how many days was it?

Must've woken up feeling better. Gone out.

All she could do was turn and go out again. The day would be endless. At the end of it would be midnight, and after that another day. The day she would be going home.

She wandered again through the rides and realized that she did not want to go on any of them, not even her favorites. She had been on them too often.

Like eating too much chocolate, I s'pose, and feeling sick.

Then she saw Ollie. She stopped dead. He was leaning up against a kiosk, looking down at something in his hands. It was the wooden doll.

Her heart flew up into her throat and beat there. She did not think; there was no time. She only knew that she must have the doll. She sped forward, snatched it in a single movement, and ran on.

"Katy! Hey, Katy!"

She ran, weaving through the crowds, and knew that he was following. She knew, too, that he would catch her. But *he can't do anything to me—not with all these people around. I'll scream!*

He caught up with her by the Corkscrew, seizing her arm. "Katy!"

"Traitor!" She spat the word at him.

"You've got it wrong."

"We thought you were our friend!"

"I *am*. You—"

"And stealing this! And don't you try to get it back! I'll scream!"

"*Listen,* will you? I didn't steal it. You dropped it."

She stared at him, confused now.

"By the stones. Lucky I got it before *he* saw it."

"But—I thought—"

"Had to play along, didn't I? What else could I do?"

"So . . . you didn't tell him? About going there, and Quantum?"

"Do me a favor. Told him I'd looked for you last night, and couldn't find you."

"Oh."

"And here—what's all this about midnight and the Black Hole?"

"So he told you! You've seen him again!"

"Wise up, will you? I told you: playing along. But better look out."

"Why?"

"Looked too pleased with himself. Like the cat that's got the cream. Said something about making sure he wasn't the only one. About taking someone with him."

"Into . . . the Black Hole?"

"Where's Josh? Is he all right?"

"Think so. I went back to the den, and he wasn't there."

Ollie frowned. "Better get back there."

"Ollie?"

He looked at her.

"You *are* on our side, aren't you?"

"Course."

"Cross your heart and hope to die?"

"*Yes.*"

"Go on—say it."

"Cross my heart and hope to die. Kids!"

She smiled, satisfied. "Sorry, Ollie."

"For what?"

"Thinking you'd pinched this."

He grinned. "Don't pinch off kids. Come on."

As they went back to the den, Katy told him of her

plan. "And I told the bag lady—Old Mother Alton. Told her to warn Quantum."

"Might work. But he's sharp. Won't just go walking in there like a lamb to the slaughter."

"He will if he thinks he can get *there*."

"We're talking big disappearance here—curtains."

"Ollie, I've seen my mum!"

"Here?" He stopped in his tracks.

"On the TV. Asking me to come home. And she's better, Ollie!"

"Good. I'm glad, kid. Home, eh?"

"I wish you'd got a home, Ollie."

"Same here, kid. But I haven't. Never will have."

"Of course you will! You will one day."

He shook his head. "Nah. Not on. One of the world's homeless, that's me."

"Oh, Ollie, poor Ollie! But if—if it works tonight, and he goes—goes for good—will you stay?"

"Dunno." He stopped and looked about him at the sunlit valley. "Might. Bit like home, now."

"Yes." She knew what he meant. It had been home to herself and Josh, too.

"You—at least you know the bag lady now."

"If you can call it knowing. Hardly saw the old bat. Any case, vanished, didn't she?"

"But she knows you're here. She'll look after you, Ollie."

"Listen," he said, "no one looks after me. No one ever has."

They reached the den and pushed their way in. It was exactly as when Katy had last seen it.

"Still not here."

Something was wrong. Josh was still poorly. He could not have gone out and stayed away so long. He had not even seemed particularly hungry. They both stood looking at the heap of belongings, as if for some clue. There was one.

"Hey!" Ollie stooped. He picked it up and it flashed in the sunlight. A silvery metal chain. "His."

"Oh, no! Oh, Ollie, I'm frightened!"

The Enemy had visited the den and taken Josh as hostage. At midnight he would enter the Black Hole, and Josh would be with him.

"Oh, he can't; he can't!"

"He will," said Ollie grimly. "Poor little devil!"

"I don't believe it! Not Josh! Oh, Josh! It's all my fault!"

"May not happen," said Ollie. "Fact, can't believe it will. A ride start up of its own accord, at midnight? *Can't.*"

"It will! Quantum will make it!"

"So now what? Try and find 'em, I s'pose. But it's hopeless. Knows this place like the back of his own hand."

"No! Go there, and tell them! We can—we've got this now." She held up the doll. "Passport."

He nodded slowly. "Call it off."

"Yes, we've got to! Or Josh—Josh—" She could not bring herself to say the words.

SEVENTEEN

"We'll go separately," Ollie said. "If he sees us together, we're done for."

"Meet just by the stones."

"And eyes peeled!" he called as he went, white-faced, yellow-haired, long-legged as a crane.

Katy watched him go, waited, then herself set off. She went fearfully, scanning about her, one hand grasping the doll in her pocket. She found herself making promises again.

If I get there safe, I'll never bite my nails again as long as I live . . . and I'll never pinch money from Mum's purse . . . and I'll practice my recorder every single night. . . .

She ran out of promises (which seemed silly and hopeless anyway) and prayed instead. *Please* let me get there, please, please!

When she reached the stones, there was no sign of Ollie.

"Ollie?" she said in a whisper.

He stepped out from among the bushes.

"Oh, Ollie!"

"Well, here goes," he said. "Got the doll?"

She showed it to him.

"I don't believe this is happening," he said.

"Ollie . . ."

He looked at her.

"Don't . . . don't be too upset if it doesn't work. For you, I mean."

"Already been there, ain't I?"

"Yes . . . but that was because of the bag lady. *She* took us. It's just that . . . well, you're not *exactly* a child, are you?"

"Never have been. Not that I remember."

"And there—the other Alton—it's a valley of children."

His face was suddenly pinched and shuttered. He shrugged. "Who cares? If they don't want me . . ."

"It's not that. *I* want you." She took his hand then, shyly, and he looked down at her, startled. "Come on, then."

And so the pair walked forward hand in hand, and with her free hand Katy again held up the doll and again whispered, "Please!" and at a certain moment heard the faint, shivering strings of the harp.

The sun still shone; the birds whistled. They stood and looked uncertainly about them.

"We're there," Katy whispered.

"Looks the same to me," he whispered back.

"No. Listen!"

"Dead quiet."

"And look!"

She pointed. They saw only trees, rising in ranks on the steep slopes, dense and secret.

"Where's *he* then? The old guy with the harp?"

"Quantum. Don't know."

Then they heard the singing.

> "Oranges and lemons
> Say the bells of St. Clemen's.
> You owe me five farthings
> Say the bells of St. Martin's."

The hidden children of the valley were at play. Katy and Ollie listened as the old words drifted up.

"*I* know that," Ollie said, and he joined softly in:

> "Here comes a candle
> To light you to bed.
> And here comes a chopper
> To chop off your head!"

He grinned sheepishly at Katy. "Forgot I knew that."

"So you were a child once."

"Must've been, I s'pose. Just don't remember."

A new game had started.

> "The farmer's in his den,
> The farmer's in his den. . . ."

"Come on—let's find them!"

And so they left the stones and went down under the layering boughs in the direction of the voices. All the while the singing grew louder, until at last they burst suddenly out of the trees into a small, sloping meadow.

There they were at last: the children, tumbling and running, dozens of them. Boys, girls—tall, short, dark, fair, all higgledy-piggledy, some in jeans, some in clothes that you only saw in films or picture books.

"I do not believe this," said Ollie again.

Then the pair were spotted, and the children ran forward, laughing and yelling. Katy saw Beth and Matt among them, and they ran to her. Ollie was seized and tugged away, half pleased and half protesting.

"Brilliant—you did it!" yelled Matt.

"No! No!"

"But I thought—"

"Where's Quantum? I must see him!"

"Gone away, o' course," said Beth in her singsong voice. "To make the song."

Katy stared. "What song?"

"For *midnight*!" Matt shouted. "Whee!" He drew great, jubilant circles in the air with his arm. "Down the spout, into outer space, done for—"

"No!" Katy screamed.

His arm dropped. "Hold on—your idea, wasn't it?"

"Yes, but it's gone wrong. He's got Josh—the Enemy's got Josh!"

"That boy? The one you were with?"

"Yes, and he told Ollie, he said if he goes he'll take someone with him. *Now* do you see?"

They looked at her, horror-struck, but said nothing.

"So take me to Quantum. Please."

Matt was shaking his head, face grave.

"What?"

"Too late. He's already made the song."

"What?"

"To make it happen. I told you—the music makes the world happen."

"But he can unmake it, can't he? He must!"

"Can't," Beth said.

"It's done, already done," Matt said. "Programmed."

The die was already cast, the wheels set in motion that would open up the dormant black hole at the stroke of midnight.

"Oh, *no!*" She was made dizzy by the realization of what she had done. "Oh, why didn't someone tell me? I don't understand—it's all such a muddle."

They stood silent, and she turned away.

"Oh, Josh!"

Josh—Mr. Fox, the ever-hungry, the brave, the survivor—would be snuffed out like a candle.

"Not your fault," said Matt awkwardly.

She whirled about. "It is! It is then! It's all my fault, and I can't bear it!"

She ran then, back into the trees. There she flung herself to the ground and sobbed.

"Oh, Josh, Josh!"

Her whole body ached with misery. She cried for ages, but the tears did not help. Usually you felt better afterward, but now she knew that rivers of tears were still there, waiting to spring up. She did not see how she could ever be happy again.

If the Enemy takes Josh into the Black Hole, I ought to go in, as well.

It was her fault. She had made the plan, and so she should take the consequences. It might not help Josh, but at least it would be fair.

She sat up, her head throbbing.

"Feeling better?"

It was Ollie, sitting nearby, nipping the seeds of grasses one by one.

She shook her head. "Did they tell you?"

"Yeah. Already programmed. Into countdown."

"Oh, I can't bear it! I'm going in as well—I've got to. But I'm frightened. What will it be like? Will I *know* I'm in a black hole? Will I—"

"Shut up. You're not going in."

"I must!"

"Fat lot of good that'd do."

"I *know*," she wailed. "But—"

"Thought you said you was going home tomorrow."

"I . . . was," she whispered.

"Well, then. Go. Least you've got a home to go to."

"I wish we'd never come here. I wish we'd never run away. I wish—"

"And a fat lot of good wishing will do. Gave up wishing a long time ago, I did. If wishing worked, we'd *none* of us be here."

The grass twisted savagely between his fingers.

"They say he'll come at dark."

She raised her head hopefully. "Quantum?"

"Yeah."

"Oh, then I can ask him—"

"Don't go getting any ideas. He can't stop it. Told you. Programmed."

"But there must be *something*. . . ."

Ollie stood up and stretched, looking about him. "Funny how this place is Alton but *not* Alton," he said. "Pity we can't stay."

"We could." Katy scrambled to her feet. "They told me. They said you can choose to stay, and Quantum makes your song, and you do!"

He gazed into the distance, chewing the grass. "Is that right?" he said, and his voice was thoughtful.

The valley slowly darkened, and still the children played in the twilit meadow. They played long after their shadows had gone and the air was chill and the dew falling. Only Katy and Ollie sat apart, with Beth and Matt.

Then flashes of light appeared in the sky, and the notes of the harp came drifting through the still air.

"Time to go," said Katy.

She and Ollie went up toward the stones, under the dark trees, and all the children in the valley followed them, solemn and whispering. At midnight they would be freed forever from the dark spell of the Enemy. But a child—a child they did not even know—must pay the price.

Quantum sat in a storm of light, bluish white erupting into the darkness. The flakes flew about him. Silently the children assembled around him, and waited.

Katy stepped forward, and again had the feeling that he sensed her presence. His fingers fell away from the strings. He turned his head.

"Well, child? Have you come to choose? Will you stay here?"

"No—no! I'm going home!"

He smiled. "Good, good."

"But it's Josh! Oh, please, sir, you've got to help him!"

The old man waited.

"Is it true that you've already made the song? For midnight and the black hole?"

"It is done. And our thanks, child, for what you have done."

"But . . . the Enemy . . . he's got Josh! And he's going to take him in there!"

Now she was looking straight into the blind, fathomless eyes.

"Save him, can't you? Save him!"

There was a silence, the silence of countless children holding their breaths.

"The song is already made. What happens in the world at midnight is already destined."

"But there must be some way! Please, please!"

He nodded slowly. "If the Enemy takes him, your friend must enter the black hole."

"Oh, no, no!"

The old man raised his hand. "Once he does so, then he is traveling backward in time."

"Oh, no, no!"

"And then, perhaps, he can be helped."

They waited, all eyes fixed on Quantum and dazzled by the storm of light.

"You have the doll?"

Silently Katy took it from her pocket and held it up.

"If your friend has it, he will be saved. It will pull him out of the stream of time and bring him here."

Another silence.

"Sir?" It was Ollie, stepping forward from the circle. "The doll. Will it bring *anyone* here, sir?"

"It will. And that is why you must be careful. If the Enemy lays hands on it, then it is he who will be brought here."

The listening children gasped and cried out in terror. Beth ran forward.

"Give it back; give it back!"

She tried to pull the doll away, but Katy tugged it free and held it behind her back.

"No, no! The Enemy won't get it! I promise!"

"You cannot promise what you do not know, child," said Quantum. "And there will be nothing I can do."

"It's mine; it's mine!" Beth tried to seize the doll again.

But now Ollie wrenched the doll from Katy's hands and held it high above his head, out of Beth's reach.

"Come on, Katy—run!"

He turned and broke through the circle of children, screaming now and clutching one another in terror. Katy, dazed, went after him.

They reached the edge of the stones, and as they did

so, Ollie turned and shouted, "'S all right! It'll be all right!"

Then he took a particular step, and Katy after him, and they were in a different night. The screams faded; the lights had gone. The pair stood, looking at each other, scared and suddenly alone. Only they, now, could play the last moves in this dangerous game. And somewhere, out there in the darkened gardens, were Josh and the Enemy, waiting for midnight.

The security men were in their office, brewing tea.

"Not a lot to do tonight, Bill."

"Not with the place swarming with cops."

"Not exactly swarming. Not tonight. Will be tomorrow, though."

"Still don't get it. If they *are* here, how come we missed 'em?"

"*Told* you I saw that girl."

"Yeah. Well."

"And the dog knew something was up. Didn't you, Prince old lad?"

The Alsatian's tail stirred feebly.

Dave glanced at the clock.

"Local news. See if we're on."

He switched on the set just as the opening music faded.

"Police say they have a new lead on the two children missing from Kirby House Children's Home since Wednesday. Two of the staff at Alton Towers have reported sightings of the girl, Katy Whittaker. It is believed that the children may have been living there and sleeping outdoors since their disappearance."

"Lose our jobs over this, if they have, the little blighters!" said Bill gloomily.

"Sh!"

A police officer appeared on the screen.

" . . . may just have been there for the day. But we are taking these sightings seriously. A small number of police with dogs will patrol the park tonight, and a full-scale search will begin at first light."

The announcer appeared again.

"We understand from an Alton Towers spokesperson that the children's mothers are already on their way there, in case—"

Dave switched off the set.

"There you go, then!" he said. "Come on—let's see if we can find 'em first."

"C'mon, Prince. You show them police dogs how to do it!"

"Quarter past eleven." Katy peered at her watch.

Moonlight shafted down on them, sitting on the crumpled heaps of clothes. "Oh, it's *still* too soon to go."

"No point going early. Only risk getting seen."

"Oh, Josh . . . I wonder what he's thinking. Or—p'r'aps he's escaped!"

"Dream on. Not a chance."

"Or the bag lady! Old Mother Alton. P'r'aps she's done something. She always—"

"Look, kid. Forget it. It's programmed, remember. It's all down to you and me."

Somewhere away in the valley an owl was hooting.

Katy shivered. "Oh, Ollie, I'm the most scared I've ever been in my whole life!"

He said nothing.

"I just can't believe this has happened. We've only been here a few days; we—oh!"

"What?"

"The calendar! I never carved it."

"You *what*?"

"We've got this calendar—notches on a tree. You know—like prisoners and hostages—and I was just carving it when the Enemy came!" She jumped to her feet.

"Where you going?"

"To carve it. Don't you see—it's bad luck. There's a day missing: today."

"So?"

"I need to carve it, for Josh."

She was already pushing her way out. Ollie followed her.

"Watch it!" he hissed. "If we're seen now, we're all sunk!"

At the calendar tree Katy started to carve the notch. As she did so, a thought struck her.

"Ollie. Midnight—is it today or tomorrow?"

"I—both, I s'pose. Does it matter?"

"Yes, because . . . I'm going to do *two* notches. This is Josh's calendar."

If she made another day for him, made tomorrow, then she, too, would be programming, in a way. She would be defying the black hole and programming a future for Josh.

Ollie shifted uneasily as she carefully carved those vital notches. "Time we went."

"Yes," she agreed. She stepped back and inspected her work, the two dark notches on the silvered bark. "That's done, then."

They turned and went back through the gardens. The whole valley was bathed in the chill light of the moon. It lay hushed, as if holding its breath. Their feet scudded softly, and now and then came the melancholy hooting of hidden owls.

They left the gardens and were for a moment exposed, in full view. They glanced swiftly to the right, where the lake lay broad and pewter. Somewhere by the entrance and the monorail, lights were flashing, blue and white.

"What is it?"

"Police—could be! Quick!"

They ran until they were in the park proper. The shortest way was past the floodlit Towers. That was too risky. They went through the Festival Park, then past the Octopus into Talbot Street. As they went past the shuttered doll museum Katy remembered that myriad of dead eyes, and shivered.

Somewhere in the valley another figure was on the move. It stepped swiftly, despite the weight in its arms. That weight was of a small boy, eyes staring up, terrified, above the thick folds of a gag. His arms were tightly bound, but his legs were free. Now and then they kicked feebly.

"Now!" hissed the Enemy exultantly as he trod toward victory. "At last!"

When he reached the Black Hole, the other two were already there in the shadows, waiting. In the full light of the moon they saw the Enemy come, with a small figure in his arms.

Katy, the doll clutched tightly, made as if to go to them, but Ollie held her back. "Wait!" he whispered.

They had already made their plan. At the moment the Black Hole started into life, as the Enemy entered, Katy would rush forward and thrust the doll into Josh's hand. It was small, and in the darkness they hoped the Enemy would not see it, would think she was simply making a last try to save her friend. It was a risky plan, and might not work, but it was all they could think of.

"And whatever happens, even if we don't get the doll to Josh, you're not to go in," Ollie had told her. He had made her promise.

The Enemy strode past so close that they could hear Josh's muffled whimpers, see the gag and his terrified eyes. They saw something else, too.

"His hands!" Katy whispered. "They're tied!"

At a stroke their plan was ruined. It was too late to make another.

As they waited, all four in the huge silence, there came a stirring. It grew to a hum, a deep throbbing.

The Black Hole was coming to life. Around them loomed the hulks of the white-knuckle rides, the Pirate Ship and Graviton, dark and silent. Only the Black Hole, powered by invisible energy, hummed and roared.

The Enemy threw back his head, triumphant; his eyes glittered in the moonlight. He stepped forward.

Then Ollie moved. He snatched the doll from Katy's grasp and sprang forward.

"No!" he shouted, and the Enemy flicked around, lips snarling.

He was taken off guard, and Ollie seized the terrified Josh, lifted him, and threw him to the ground.

"*I'll* go!"

But Katy had seen something else go flying through the air.

"The doll!"

She ran past the desperately writhing Josh and picked it up.

By now Ollie and the Enemy were on the very threshold of the Black Hole. Katy ran and thrust the doll at Ollie. But the Enemy saw her.

"What's *that*?"

Ollie tried to hide it, but too late. Next moment the pair were locked in a deadly struggle for possession of the doll.

"Ollie! Ollie!" It was Josh, who had pulled away his gag and struggled to his knees.

Katy ran forward and pummeled the Enemy

with her fists. Ollie and the Enemy fought and swayed. Behind them the Black Hole hammered and roared.

Then, as if losing balance together, they staggered into the entrance. One minute they were there, clearly visible in the moonlight, the next swallowed into the dark.

Katy screamed. "No!"

She stood, desperate. Again she screamed.

The power was gathering; the domed cover seemed to quiver with its force. In there, still locked in combat, Ollie and the Enemy were finally entering the black hole. And at the moment they entered it, only one would be holding that rough wooden doll.

One would go spinning to that other Alton, to the world of Quantum and the golden harp whose music made the world happen. The other would plunge into a fathomless void.

The noise was deafening now, no ordinary grind of machinery. A hole was being torn in the fabric of the world itself, in time and space. Josh and Katy crouched, hands covering their ears, terrified.

Then came a whirlwind, a mighty rush of icy air that flattened their hair, forced open their eyelids. It roared and swirled and screamed as if to suck them, too, into its vortex, and they screamed, soundlessly, their breath driven back into their lungs. It was as if they were drowning.

Then, just as they felt they might shatter under the

force of it, the wind went spiraling back in narrowing circles, back into its center in the black hole. Their breathing eased; the roar faded.

Then there was silence.

EPILOGUE

That is all. Josh and Katy were still crouching there, ears ringing, stunned, when the police patrol found them, quite by chance. No one at Alton Towers that night had seen or heard anything unusual.

The children's obvious terror was put down as natural—that and their hysterical sobbing as they were reunited with their mothers.

Josh and Katy never told the whole story of their time at Alton Towers. No one would have believed them. Who would believe in a lost valley of children, shepherded there over the centuries by a bag lady? In Quantum, fingering the golden harp whose music makes the world happen? Ollie and the Enemy, homeless and drifting, did not exist, as far as the world was concerned. As Ollie himself had said, they were not minors. No one missed them.

And no one knows, of course, what happened—might still be happening—in the black hole. No one has ever been in a black hole and returned to tell the story. Katy and Josh would hope against hope that Ollie had won the fight and was now in that other Alton, at home at last, while the Enemy had gone screaming into the pit.

Or were the pair in a kind of limbo, still wrestling for possession of the carved doll that was their only hold upon time itself?

The worst nightmare was the one neither of them ever put into words, even to each other: that the Enemy finally won the doll and that Ollie, their brave friend, was the one sucked into oblivion.

Then the Enemy would have become king again, master of the harp and the black hole. He would be there, playing a cruel game of cat and mouse, waiting his chances.

And then one day, one perfectly ordinary day at Alton Towers under a clear blue sky, unsuspecting children would stand lining up to disappear forever. . . .